Highland Journey

Doug Godsman

ISBN: 978-0-578-71502-5

Dedication

To Phyllis, for her long-suffering, lip-biting support during the creative process! Without her, this book would not have seen the light of day.

To Jen and Neil, my children, the best people with the biggest hearts.

And,

To Readers, Authors, Writers, Bloggers, Journalers, Book Groups, and Writing Groups everywhere. Society needs the written word. Your contribution is invaluable. Thank you!

Part 1

"An honest Man's the
noblest work of God."

"The Cottar's
Saturday Night"
Robert Burns

In 1905, before "Highland Journey" … Why?

Sir David Rennie:

"Why do we keep meeting, then separating? Our meeting at the street party in Ballboyne, for example. Bella left on the next morning's train to Glasgow and the boat from Scotland to America."

Bella Gordon:

"Why does David continue to rescue me from the Lederbeiter clan? First the assault by Wilhelm Lederbeiter on the liner. Then at Ellis Island where Wilhelm's sister kidnapped me to work in her brothel."

David and Bella:

"Why was our only time alone together so short? We could have kissed forever."

Bella:

"Why did Baron Tookov choose to swindle David's father, Lord Rennie, using a silver mine in Arkansas as bait?"

David:

"Why is Bella taking the train to San Francisco and I'm not?"

David and Bella:

"When will we see each other again?"

Chapter 1

Bella screamed.

Her brother George shot up and smashed his skull on the slats underneath her bunk. Mr. Pullman's carriages were luxurious, but, in 1905, unduly small for a large Scottish lad.

"Bella! Bella! You're safe! It's me, it's George. Ah, ye puir wee lamb. You're having a nightmare is all. Here, let me hold you. I've got you. You're safe." He wasn't used to consoling lassies, even his own sister, but holding her and soft talk seemed to do the trick.

"Are you okay, Bella? It was an awfie dream by the sound of it. What were you dreaming?"

"It was terrible, George, terrible! I was on the ship and the Lederbeiters chased me into the Ellis Island infirmary with the typhoid patients and Sir David was there."

"Sir David!" George pulled back and squinted at Bella. "Did he put his hands on you?"

"No, he was trying to rescue me, but the Lederbeiters had him handcuffed and they were evicting me in my undies! Oh, my dream's mixed up, but it scared the dickens out of me because I couldn't free David." She drew a deep breath.

The big man was a practical, hard-headed Scot who had trouble remembering the act of dreaming, never mind the details. Bella's description made little sense to him, but he realized the talking dulled her terror. He wanted Bella to carry on but they were interrupted by a thunderous knock on the compartment door.

"Mr. Gordon, Miss Gordon, what's going on in there? We heard screaming."

Bella grinned at her brother and giggled. "Oops! They think I'm being murdered! Wait a moment, please." She wrapped a blanket round her, then motioned to George to open the door of their sleeping chamber. There stood the porter and another passenger, their neighbor no doubt.

George pre-empted their complaint. "We're sorry to wake you. My sister here had a terrible dream and screamed. As you can see, she's fine." He stepped away to show Bella draped in her blanket.

"My apologies, gentlemen. My brother's correct, I'm fine now." Her brilliant smile won over the visitors in an instant.

"We wanted to check that you're all right, miss. It was one heck of a scream."

"Yes," thought Bella, *"If you only knew."*

The porter escorted the neighbor back to his cabin and George locked up behind them. "Weel, Sis, it'll soon be daylight and I won't sleep any more. What do you say I put on my clothes and rustle up a cup of tea? Or, better still, how'd you like a coffee?!"

"I'll not sleep again either, George, and I'd enjoy a coffee, thank you. I'll dress while you go rustling!"

*   *   *

"Bella, are you all right, for sure? You've been through a lot." George mumbled through a mouthful of muffin. "You look pale and worn, and your spark's missing."

Bella sighed, exasperated at her brother's smothering mothering and not wanting to reflect on herself any more. She had spent most of the journey from New York chewing over her future. "I know you have my best interests at heart, George, but I wish you'd leave me be for a wee while. We arrive in Chicago soon and change trains, don't we? Let's talk afterwards. There'll be lots of time."

"Very well, Sis, we'll wait."

"Remember to send a telegram to Ma and Pa telling them our arrival time at Oakland. Are you able to do that?"

"Not yet, this new technical stuff is fair baffling me, but I'll manage."

*   *   *

Bella was correct; they had oodles of opportunities to visit. The train journey from Chicago to Omaha, Nebraska, on to Ogden, Utah, and to their final destinations, Oakland and San Francisco, took eight days.

"Weel, Bella, tell me what's on your mind."

"Oh George! Everything and nothing. I'm confused. Remember our last night in Ballboyne when we sat on the wall and how excited we were to be emigrating from Scotland to California? The next day I was concerned what my life would be like there. Then Da, of all people, told me about the blank canvas and how I'd paint my own future on it? Well, all that's happened since has changed that plan."

George nodded in encouragement.

"I was looking forward to our family putting down roots and building a home and me being a teacher or even a tutor. Now all I can think of is David and how much I want to be with him." Bella colored, but the implication sailed over George's head.

"Aye, lassie, he has done us many a good turn. I'll always be grateful to him for saving you from the Lederbeiters. He's no' a bad bloke despite being a swell."

Bella took a swipe at his arm, a smile ghosting across her face. Her brother continued; "But remember what I told you at the farewell party back in Ballboyne? The gentry only become serious with their own kind? He's a decent man, but still gentry. He can't be that different."

Bella reflected on the conversation and kisses she and her rescuer had shared in the carriage as they circled Central Park. *Oh yes, he's different!* She touched her fingers to her lips, smiled at the memory and gazed out of the window, seeing only darkness. Then she remembered their last words on the Penn Street station platform. *"Come for me, David," she had insisted, "Find me!"*

"Perhaps you're correct, George. He didn't reply when I asked him—no, demanded—he find me." Bella sniffled into her hankie.

George would have preferred to stick his head in a wasp's nest than have this discussion. But he hated to see his sister so upset. And, though David was nobility, he was a male, and so deserved some of George's support. "You're right, Bella; he didna answer. But he also said he never made promises he couldn't keep. To me, it sounded as though he would have liked to have promised you. Don't give up hope yet!"

Bella stared at him with surprise. "He did say that, didn't he? George, times, you amaze me!" She sat up straighter. "I must have faith in him. My heart tells me we're meant to be together, which means he'll find me. I don't know where and I don't know when, but he'll find me, that I know. Thanks, George, you're a blessing!" Her brother tolerated another hug.

Chapter 2

Sir David Rennie nursed a fine Glenfiddich in his suite at the Waldorf-Astoria, second-guessing himself.

I should have gone with her! Damn family, damn duty, I want to spend the rest of my life with her. Why did she leave and I didn't?

His mind slipped back to their farewell on the platform at the Penn Street Station, the desperate kisses, the eyes, her eyes, beseeching him to find her in San Francisco, the train gathering itself like a huge dragon, puffing and smoking and inching forward, then gathering speed. He had waved and waved again; positive he could see her small white handkerchief fluttering in response. The train chugged around a corner, the lovers' view interrupted, but for how long? Forever? There were few certainties in 1905.

Tam McKenzie, Sir David's ex-military bodyguard and friend, nudged David back into the present. "Would you care for another whisky, Sire?"

David sighed. "No thanks, Tam. I have my appointment at the British Trade Commission at ten, I'd better not show up having finished the bottle tonight."

Wallowing in his misery looked very attractive to him at the moment, but he shook himself and became all business again.

"First, I need to trace the swindler who stole the family fortune." David's voice hardened. "I can't wait to confront Baron Pyotr Tookov or Peter Thomas or whatever he calls himself today. He's due a day of reckoning and I'm looking forward to obliging him. Finding him must take precedence over affairs of the heart - it's my duty to my family. The sooner I confront him, the sooner I can find Bella." His thoughts drifted west, towards his love, but he pulled his mind back to his immediate concerns. "I'm off to bed, Tam. Goodnight."

Tam left the suite to check on the Pinkerton men David had hired to guard him on his arrival from Scotland, was it merely two days ago? So much had happened, not only saving Bella from the brothel but protecting David from muggings, knifings and shootings here in New York. Baron Tookov must be serious about stopping Sir David. The Scots were eager to find out why.

Chapter 3

"Let me get this straight," Ewan Campbell hopped from boot to boot. "You want me to get rid of a Scottish Lord?" He couldn't keep the delight out of his deep bass voice, so well-suited to his six-foot three inch, 220-pound frame.

"Yeah, well, the offspring of a Lord, Sir David Rennie. Why are you so interested in who he is? How come you're so chatty?" Mario Gamborini stared at Ewan, who'd never let more than two words come out of his mouth in their previous meetings. They were in the back room of Gamborini's Little Italy trattoria, hidden from the general populace by a lattice wall interlaced with climbing vines struggling for life. Gamborini sipped a chianti, Campbell a cola.

Campbell clamped down onto his tongue, he'd said enough. "When? How much?"

"I need him dead yesterday. Three of my men tried to kill him but failed and the client, Baron Tookov, is getting impatient. I'll give you $100 once you've done him in. That's twice your usual. Agreed?"

100 dollars?! They must really need this son-of-a-lord dead. Whoever 'they' is. Ewan nodded. "I'm okay with that. How do I find him?"

"He's staying at the Waldorf-Astoria. He has a bodyguard, Tam McKenzie, an ex-military man who's big and competent. Rennie's surrounded by Pinkerton men too, so it won't be a picnic."

Campbell's enthusiasm wasn't the least diminished. "I'll find a way."

Gamborini believed him. Despite his youth, Campbell was the premier hit man in New York with an impressive string of kills.

*   *   *

Ewan Campbell was a changed man when he left Gamborini's trattoria. Hidden beneath his natural taciturn demeanor was a childish delight. *I get to kill a Lord! I get to kill a Lord!* He caught himself dancing up the alleyway but slowed and returned to his normal, self-effacing shuffle. *Don't attract attention. Not now. Still, $100, that's double my normal fee.* He hopped on a streetcar going in the right direction, changing several times before ending up on Park Avenue opposite David Rennie's luxurious hotel. The streetcar rides afforded him plenty of time to reflect on his good fortune. *At last, I'll avenge my* *parents, may they rest in peace. I know this David Rennie had nothing to do with their deaths, but his bloody ruling class did, and I'll take my revenge on him.*

He crossed the Avenue, checking for anyone trailing him. *No, I'm alone.*

He gulped as he remembered the sad chain of events leading up to his being orphaned: the false accusations against his father by the Glasgow Lord's promiscuous daughter; the subsequent beating which left his Da a hollow shell of a man until he died three months later; the same Lord then attacking his mother. "Tit-for-tat," Lord Gorbals had said while fending off the eight-year-old Ewan. The nobleman even evicted them from their cottage on the estate, but Ewan took his revenge. He stole the noble's prize shotguns and pawned them to buy immigrant tickets to New York.

Sad to say, the New World had treated his mother worse than Scotland had. She succumbed to drink within the year, leaving Ewan to join a mob of scrappy, dirty urchins fending for themselves on the streets. His survival was desperate until puberty gifted him with big strong bones which, when coupled with a ferocious anger, made people avoid him. He'd joined a gang... not that he'd had a choice. Ewan started as a numbers runner, but after he bulked up, he'd moved into collection, then enforcement and finally to the top job, liquidation. He was without emotion, was ruthless, inventive and focused.

From an alcove across the street, Campbell watched the comings and goings at the hotel's grand entrance, marveling at how easy it was to gain access. *But once I'm inside, how will I kill him?*

Chapter 4

C ampbell was a well-dressed assassin, nice suit, matching homburg, good shoes. He had no trouble slipping by the Pinkerton men and strolling into the Waldorf-Astoria's foyer. The dinner crowd had thinned, but enough patrons remained in the foyer to provide cover as he loitered by the concierge's desk. Thirty minutes into his vigil, a large take-charge kind of man, not quite a gentleman but wearing a suit cut in the British fashion, approached the concierge. With a bounce in his walk and a gleam in his eye, it was Tam McKenzie.

*   *   *

Tam inspected the concierge's name tag. "Antoine, where is the nearest semi-respectable bar with live music?"

Antoine hadn't arrived at his premier concierge position in New York without learning to size up his clientele. "Mr. McKenzie, isn't it? Ah, yes sir, good food, strong ales and the possibility of meeting a companion for the night. Am I right?"

Tam smiled. "Yes, Antoine, you have me pegged."

"There are two places I can recommend." He gave Tam clear directions, but Ewan stopped listening to the conversation.

What luck! It sounds as though Mackenzie'll be away all night, leaving Rennie by himself. Better and better!

Tam waved a cheery goodbye to Antoine and stepped outside to give the Pinkerton guards their final instructions.

Ewan grabbed the concierge. "Was that Mister McKenzie I missed?"

"Yes, sir, it was."

"Damn, I have a message for his employer. Is Sir David still on the top floor, suite 1705?"

"Yes sir, he's on the top floor, but not 1705." Five and ten-dollar bills changed hands. "You may want to try 1715, Mister..."

"Perceval, Jonah Perceval. Thank you, Antoine."

*　　*　　*

Ewan strode past the bank of elevators to the bar. An idea for Sir David's demise flirted with the edges of his mind, and he fleshed out the details while sipping a Coke. *Yes, this will work and be a spectacle, for sure. Time's a passing, I need to complete this before McKenzie gets back.*

"Barkeep! Give me a bottle of your best champagne, will you. Charge it to my room, 1715. My name's Rennie."

Armed with his expensive bottle, Ewan entered the elevator farthest from the lobby, the one least-used. He told the elevator operator, an old-timer called Walter, to take him to the fourteenth floor. He exited left to the stairs at the end of the corridor and climbed the remaining three floors. Before entering this corridor, he grabbed the long-handled emergency axe from its clamp on the wall and hid it under his coat. No one was in view when he peeked out, nor when he hurried to the elevator bank. He pushed the button and held his breath, hoping for the same elevator to return.

Walter showed no surprise that a client had got off at one floor and re-entered on another. He had seen everything during his 24 years of service, so this was a minor item. Why he could tell you stories...

and Ewan hit him flush on the temple and Walter crumpled like an ill-made souffle.

The elevator doors were closing when Ewan jammed the fire axe between them, wedging them half-open. He grasped the operator by the collar and heaved him into the corridor. Campbell over-rode the safety switch, sent the empty elevator to the basement, then dragged Walter to the stairwell. He looked as though he would be out cold for a long time. Ewan pulled off his overcoat and homburg, leaving them with Walter before easing himself back into the hallway. He straightened his jacket and smoothed his hair, picked up the champagne and knocked on David's door.

"Who's there?"

"It's Jonah Perceval, Sir David. I'm the manager of the hotel and I have a gift to welcome you to the Waldorf-Astoria."

"A gift, you say?" David cracked the door, keeping his foot close behind it.

"Yes, Sir, we have an excellent wine cellar and this bottle is one of our best, an 1866 Dom Perignon." Ewan held out the bottle for David's inspection.

David opened the door to inspect the gift. "That's kind of..." He got no further. Ewan grabbed the lapels of David's jacket, head-butted him, and pulled him towards the gaping elevator shaft.

David was dazed but still had enough sensibility to realize what his future held when he saw the open elevator door but no elevator. *What had Tam taught me? Use the element of surprise, do the unexpected.* He shouted for help at the top of his lungs, dropped to his knees and twisted his body. David's contortions broke Ewan's initial grasp but ended up much worse off because Ewan pulled him into a headlock from the rear.

Got him! thought Ewan. *Let's get him over to the elevator shaft and it's goodbye, Sir David.* Ewan tightened his forearm around David's neck, lifted him off the floor and shuffled towards the elevator door.

David could see he was running out of time and options, but another of Tam's tricks forced its way into his consciousness. He tugged on Ewan's arm, the arm that was carrying him and, now, suffocating him.

When Campbell responded by tightening his grip, David came close to blacking out. He was two feet from the threshold of the elevator shaft.

David stuck his right foot forward, then lashed backwards as hard as he could. His hard leather heel connected with Ewan's shin, which sent excruciating pain shooting through his attacker's right leg. Ewan relaxed his grip, loosened his arm, and tried to hop on his left leg.

When David's feet found the floor, he took advantage of Ewan's imbalance by lunging forward at the waist, hanging onto Ewan's forearm as he did so. Ewan somersaulted over David's head... and disappeared into the shaft. He proclaimed his displeasure for the next 14 floors. Then a "whump". Then quiet.

*   *   *

David sat with his back to the wall, gasping for breath, happy that it wasn't his last.

Doors had opened, guests who had heard the commotion stood in various stages of undress, watching the drama unfold. Hotel security, management, police, then Tam arrived, summoned by a message from Antoine. Walter emerged from the stairwell and corroborated David's story. He wasn't unconscious, as Ewan had thought, and had watched the struggle from afar. The police reaction was noteworthy. Here was a foreign noble ridding

New York of one of its most wanted criminals. How much energy were they expected to spend on David, other than thanking him again and again?

Tam was distraught, angry, guilty and in shock. Distraught because of how close Campbell had come to succeeding, angry at David for falling for such a simple trick, at himself for not being a better teacher to his ward and guilty because his one responsibility was to keep Sir David alive and well. Later that night, after the police had left, David and Tam shared a good malt whisky. When Tam tried again to apologize, David dismissed the notion.

"Tam, it was me that was stupid enough to open the door. I deserved everything I got, and it's not your fault. In fact, it's because of your teaching that I survived. Now, I'm older and wiser and better prepared. Yes, it might have been a disaster, but it wasn't. What is it you always tell me? Forget the couldabeens, focus on this moment? We must keep our guard up, because Tookov isn't relenting. What's he protecting? Something more than just an investment scam?"

Tam nodded in agreement. "You're right, Sire. Off to St. Louis tomorrow. What's next, I wonder? Will Tookov still be there?"

Chapter 5

David had endured the trip from New York to St. Louis as best he could, Tam watching with paternal affection. *Ah yes, the sweetness and sorrow of first love!* Tam had long forgotten his initial love, but he'd caused enough heartache and suffering among the opposite sex to recognize a severe case of puppy love when he saw it. He knew that telling David to "Snap out of it!" or "Grow up!" or "You'll get over it!" would be an exercise in futility. To give David his due, he didn't mope or sulk or beat his breast crying "Woe is me!" Rather, he became quiet and introspective. It was obvious he was reminiscing over his time with Bella. Tam noticed David was touching his lips, perhaps remembering the kisses that had set them on fire.

Tam interfered only once. After changing trains in Chicago, Tam said, "Sir David, I can't say I know how you feel, only you know that. But it's easy to allow grief to consume you. May I suggest you set a timetable to limit how long you'll grieve? You'll always remember Bella, but meantime we have other fish to fry, important to your family."

David raised bloodshot eyes; sleep was hard to come by these days. "You're right as usual, Tam." He sighed. "I need to come to terms with what happened between us. And I must also focus on Tookov or Thomas fellow." His voice strengthened. "Right, I'll be back in form before St. Louis. And, Tam, kick my arse if I backslide."

There. A glimmer of a smile. Tam grinned. "You can count on me, Sir!"

David continued, "My mind hasn't been exclusive to Bella. I've been thinking of Tookov and my Evening Star mine as well. The sooner we arrive in Rush, the happier I'll be. I wish I could tell how large a lead Tookov enjoys. I must stop him from tampering with the ownership of the Evening Star."

Tam grunted in understanding.

"Another thing, you'll remember when we left Ballboyne, I asked you to drop the formality and you've done a good job. But America is more informal than I imagined. If we're to appear as colleagues, call me David."

Tam swallowed; this was breaking all the rules of British society. "Thank you, sire, that's a huge honor. I'd be happy to... David!"

"Which leads me to fitting into our surroundings better. Our clothes make us stick out like swans at a funeral of crows. It'll be even more pronounced when we arrive in Arkansas. I doubt there'll be many miners who buy their working wear from bespoke tailors in Savile Row!"

Tam smiled. "I agree, David. Let me buy workmen's clothes before we leave St Louis. And, rather than traveling first class, let's mix with the third-class."

"Good idea, Tam, but rather than new duds, find broken-in overalls."

"Right, 'experienced' clothes it is! And now I understand why peach fuzz is growing on your cheeks. A beard makes sense."

David even laughed. "One last thing, Tam. Ask how we get to Rush and what to expect when we arrive. It's a dark unknown and I'm curious to know ahead of time what we might find."

Tam left to chat up other passengers while David tried to sink back into melancholy. But talking with

Tam had had its effect. He looked forward instead of back, a sure cure for depression.

*   *   *

Tam returned from his fact-finding mission a few minutes before dinner. "Well, David, I have a rough idea of what to expect once we're in the country, and I do mean rough. Travel by horseback in the hills of Arkansas is close to impossible because of the poor state of the roads. It'd take a whole day to move fifteen miles while the steamboats can cover up to twenty miles in an hour, depending on the water conditions."

"Ah, keep to the rivers as much as possible. Good. What else?"

"We're entering a harsh part of the world, David. The riverboats have a staggering reputation for lawlessness and violence. Most mining camps are wild, and aimless drifters roam nearby causing trouble. We'll have to keep our wits about us."

David cracked a weak grin. "Sounds like Saturday nights in Glasgow. Very well, add guns to your list of purchases. Anything else?"

"We might go by land later, but I must impress on you how poor this country is with no lodgings for travelers such as ourselves. If we must travel overland, we'll be roughing it."

"Better and better!"

"How so, David?"

"I expect we're more able to rough it than our friend Tookov, don't you think?"

Chapter 6

A thousand miles to the south, Baron Pyotr Tookov, alias Peter Thomas, the Cockney scam artist from London's Cheapside, knocked his son, Corporal Michael Thomas, to the floor and kicked him hard in the ribs.

"I gave you one thing to do!"

Kick.

"Keep that damned son of Lord Rennie away from America!"

Kick.

"You can't even do that right!" Tookov was screaming now. Michael curled his six-foot frame into a ball, protecting his head and other vital parts of his body.

Kick.

Thomas was ten inches shorter than his son, but years of practice allowed him to deliver a solid wallop.

"Get up! Get up, I said!"

The corporal refused, knowing first-hand his father would beat him down again. Instead he rolled away, hiding among the furniture in the best suite in St. Louis' best hotel, The Union Station. Michael's face was a picture of humiliation mixed with pure, white-hot hatred.

Tookov couldn't manage a clear kick at his boy but continued his harangue. "Why didn't you finish him while you had the chance? You could have tried a second time? Or a third? And, for crying out loud, why did you take a different ship to America? You'd have had a dozen opportunities a day to do him in if you'd been on the same boat!"

The younger Thomas kept silent, knowing from experience Senior didn't want logical answers to his emotional outburst. He wouldn't listen to his son's explanations anyhow. That was his father's way, a painful way to be sure, and he was sick and tired of the abuse. How much more of this could he take? He'd been on the receiving end of his parent's temper for years, and he'd had enough. He risked a glance at the big satchel visible in the wardrobe of his dad's bedroom. "There's my future." he thought.

Thomas the elder kept on whining. "I've had to pull out of New York, the city with the easiest marks in the world. Pinkertons have been sniffing around, thanks to Lord la-de-da Rennie. Now his bloody son is on his way, because you were too sissified to handle a simple murder. I'll tell you something: your brother, bless his soul, would have done it in no time flat and done it right. Gorblimey, I miss him."

That was it. Michael couldn't stand to hear once again how inferior he was to his dead sibling Jack. He snapped and screamed back.

"You great big bag of wind! Whenever things don't go your way, I get the blame and you hold your sainted son Jack up as the shining star. Huh! If Jack was so bloody smart, how come he's dead, then?" Michael wasn't a mimic like his father, so his accent was pure London east end cockney. "A rival gang jumped him back in London, right? Jack shouldn't have been on their turf. Looking for a piece of skirt, wasn't he? Serve him bleeding right. And as for David bloody Rennie, Jack would've done the same as me."

Michael's outburst astounded Thomas Senior... his son never talked back. He lunged for Michael, but the corporal put the Baby Grand between them. Senior's anger had now reached homicidal proportions.

The corporal made his choice: he'd get out from under his father's abuse. He'd disappear with the satchel full of bearer bonds bought with the proceeds of his father's various scams.

The Count gave up chasing Michael and raged around the hotel room, kicking everything he could reach, often to his own detriment. On a good day, he appeared genial, smooth and suave, but not today. His volcanic outburst was distorting his face into something akin to a Bosch painting of hell. His east end accent had returned, no more the urbane, knowledgeable, international investor, just another swindler feeling the noose tightening.

Then, just as quickly as he had blown up, it was over, and he got back to business. "Listen, I've arranged for thugs in New York to fix David bloody Rennie once and for all. We need to hurry to Rush to change the mine registration so we own it, not Lord Rennie. I'm sure if we grease enough fat palms, we can manage that."

"Why own a mine? I thought the plan was to set up in Washington and fleece investors as usual?"

"Didn't you see the American Miners Journal report? It said there's the possibility of a sizable body of ore and it might be worth millions. That's why. Must Rush be such an out-of-the-way place? Arkansas, for heaven's sake! What kind of name is that anyway? It'll be days before we get there. Now, here's what I want you to do..."

Chapter 7

Western Union

BARON PYOTR TOOKOV UNION STATION HOTEL ST LOUIS MISSOURI STOP ONE MAN DEAD THREE INJURED STOP SEND MORE MONEY TO DEAL WITH TARGET STOP GAMBORINI

Tookov/Thomas exploded again. "What the hell does he mean, "Send more money"? I gave him plenty to fix David bedamned Rennie. So what if he's lost men, that's his problem!" Thomas Senior was pacing and booting everything in sight. "He's trying to squeeze me! To hell with him! He's getting nothing more from me. To hell with him, you hear?"

Corporal Thomas stepped out of his father's path of destruction. "He could be telling the truth. Rennie might be here already. He's a capable man, and he's got that big servant with him, the ex-soldier. Formidable, I'd say." Michael loved to wind his father up, now that he'd decided to scarper with the satchel and its contents,

Thomas Senior paused for a protracted moment, which showed something was seriously wrong. Before today, his intellect was his strongest asset... quick, insightful and decisive. The stress of being on the run with justice catching up was affecting him. He was drinking more, sleeping less, gorging himself at the table. Usually, his immaculate clothing identified him: it was part of his con. But today, his suits were crumpled and stained ... they'd even been slept in. He wouldn't have impressed his Park Avenue marks today. But his mind showed the greatest degradation. He took too long to make the simplest decisions and, when he chose a course of action, he'd reverse himself over and over. He was falling apart.

"Do you think so?" he said. "He could be in St. Louis?"

"They might be in that crowd!" Corporal Thomas peered through the curtains of the window, smiling to himself.

Thomas Senior took the bait and rushed to his son's side, scanning with dread the station's Grand Hall below. "How would I recognize him?"

"You know, British. Well-dressed, clean-shaven, well-fed, healthy. Stand out like a sore thumb. He's in his early twenties, tall, black hair, green eyes. His man's in his forties and fit too, but thicker, stronger.

He has an air of experience and competence. Not someone to underestimate."

Senior paled even more. "What do I do? What do I do?"

His son thought of the bearer bonds and the mine. *Should I steal the satchel now and make my escape? Or should I wait for the big prize, ownership of the Evening Star?* Greed beat prudence yet again. "Here, Da, I've bought the tickets to Batesville. Let's go. They'll never find you in Arkansas."

"Where's Batesville? What of our luggage? Should we take it with us?" And the indecisiveness blazed through.

"Batesville's on the way to Rush and the mine. The baggage is under control. Come on, we can't miss the train."

Thomas Senior had shaken off his mental fog and was back to his normal self. He led his son and the porter with their luggage through Union Station's Grand Hall. He ignored the magnificent stained-glass windows and 65-foot barrel-vaulted ceiling soaring over the mosaic floor; Thomas took little notice of his surroundings unless there was something in it for him. Then again, if he'd realized the gilding on the arches was gold leaf, he might have paid more attention.

The crowd in the Hall was huge: a large slice of America in one room and on the move. The sixteen platforms disgorged thousands of passengers each day. Workers, families, immigrants, travelers, the masses spoke, shouted or whispered in a hundred tongues. Men wore their blue, brown or black suits and work clothes with matching homburgs or fedoras, caps or top hats, the monochrome relieved by a muted hue from their neckerchiefs. The women, old and young, all shapes and sizes, stylish or frumpy, brought life and vibrancy and vitality to the multitude with accessories of every color in the rainbow.

The Thomases joined the throng. "Son, here's your ticket, tell the porter to take our gear to our cabin. I'll settle our bill."

"All right, Da, I'll wait for you onboard." Junior watched the valise disappear into the crowd, expecting to see it—and his father—again, but not one hundred percent convinced. However, he followed their baggage to the Iron Mountain Railway platform.

Chapter 8

Thomas Senior haggled with the front desk about his bill. He complained of the service and the lumps in the bed and the lack of amenities. None of this was true, of course, but squeezing the last penny out of any transaction was his basic tenet. Finally, to get rid of him, the Reception Manager took ten percent from the total and sent him on his way. The hotelier also ensured that the name, Baron Tookov, appeared at the top of the black list. The hotel wouldn't turn him aside but, next time he showed, the receptionist would allot him the least desirable room, the one near Mr. Otis's squeaky elevator where the hot water ran on occasion and was within eyesight, earshot and bovine whiff of the stockyards.

Thomas Senior was congratulating himself on his negotiation skills when he saw the time on the ornate clock in the Grand Hall. *Damn, I'll miss my train if I don't hurry!* He stepped up his pace and plowed through the crowd like a bull at Pamplona. He knocked several people aside and one old man to the ground before a large gentleman seized him. "Steady on, there, you'll hurt someone."

Thomas had a sharp retort ready when the accent stopped him. *Scottish? Is this…?* He peered at the big man's companion. *Tall, black hair, green eyes. Gorblimey! It's him! It's them!* His knees turned to spaghetti and his mouth to mush. No coherent words formed. He tore his arm out of Tam's grasp and dashed off, barreling through the crowd even faster, again leaving pain, anger and brandished fists in his wake. Tam and David shook their heads and continued to the hotel.

Thomas Senior found the Iron Mountain gate and rushed pell-mell towards the railcar and the illusionary safety of his cabin. Junior scanned the platform, concerned that his father, or, more to the point, the satchel, might be too late.

Senior launched himself onto the stairs and pushed Michael along the corridor to their berth. "It's them, Son! It's them!"

"Calm down, Da. Who's 'them'?"

"Rennie! Sir David bloody Rennie and his man. They're here. I ran into them in the Hall. I ran right into them. Oh, they'll catch us, I know it!"

"How did you recognize them? You've never seen each other."

"The big fellow grabbed me and told me to go slower. He had a Scots brogue and was in his forties, as you described. Rennie was there, dark hair and green eyes, but he's started a beard."

"What happened after that, Da?"

"I broke free and rushed away from them." Thomas Senior shivered. Thomas Junior was thinking fast.

"Did you speak to them?"

"What? No. Why?"

"They've never seen you, have they? Your accent is all that identifies you. We don't have anything to worry about. You're confident you said nothing?"

"Positive." Thomas Senior relaxed as his son's logic penetrated his fuzzy brain.

"Right, then, we're fine. I'll keep an eye open until we leave." He stuck his head out the window and searched the crowds.

Thomas Senior took his seat and examined Michael. *He's grown. Those few months in the army have done him good. His thinking is crisp, he takes charge when necessary. He's even filled out; I wouldn't want to meet him on a dark night in an alley. Good for him. And good for me, since it looks as though I'm going to need muscle to protect my assets.* He paused. *I should change that to 'our' investments.* He patted his precious satchel with his right hand while clutching it more tightly with his left.

Thomas Senior had cut it close. The conductor blew his whistle, the porters pulled in their steps and the locomotive set off hissing, steaming and smoking.

Thomas Junior pulled back into the carriage. "No sign of them, but I'll walk through the cars and make sure they're not on board."

"But won't Sir David recognize you? Didn't he see you when you attacked him in Glasgow?"

"Nah, I came at him from behind. He's no idea of what I look like. If I spot him, I'll turn around and come back. I'll keep my mouth shut too, so they can't hear my cockney. It'd be best if you stay put until I've had a gander."

Chapter 9

David and Tam disembarked from their train and followed their luggage through the St. Louis train depot, marveling at the surrounding architecture. They were halfway to their hotel when a small, barrel-shaped gent ran into them. He was bulldozing his way through the crowd without thought of the chaos he was leaving.

Tam seized the little man's arms. "Steady on there, you'll hurt someone!" The human plow glared at Tam, then David. He turned white, tore free and rushed towards the platforms even quicker, clutching his briefcase to his chest.

Tam and David looked at each other, could make nothing of it, and shrugged their shoulders. "He must have spied a ghost," muttered Tam. The pair continued into the Union Station Hotel.

The manager was John Sutherland, a florid southerner of middle height and nearing 30. He worked long hours for his establishment, and it showed. He was flabby, unhealthy and pale from enjoying little sunlight. As the Scots approached the reception desk, they found him bent over, holding his hands to his aching gut. Thanks to Thomas, stress had struck, sending knives of pain into his belly and making it hard for him to function. But when he noticed the quality of his new guests' clothes, he straightened up and donned his most welcoming smile.

Once the formalities were over and the hotel's services explained, David asked, "By the way, is there a Baron Tookov registered?"

The transformation in the manager's demeanor was visible. He changed from a friendly, open, cooperative administrator, to a rigid, formal, aloof, almost French, clerk. "Is he a friend of yours, sir?" The ice in his voice was palpable.

"Quite the reverse, he's no friend of mine."

Sutherland picked up on David's matching frosty tone. He relaxed and pulled on his helpful persona again. "Thank goodness, I've had enough of his ilk today. He checked out not two minutes ago. You must have passed him at the entrance."

Tam put it together. "A short, stubby man wearing a good gray suit and clutching a black leather satchel?"

"That's him!"

"Which platform for the trains to Batesville?"

"Track six." The manager glanced at the clock. "It's just leaving, though."

The compatriots ran out into the Great Hall, trying not to bull people aside like Thomas, scanning the departure boards for platform six, desperate to collar Thomas before he left. But it was not to be. When they located the correct platform, the tail of the train was disappearing around a bend.

Tam grabbed a porter. "Excuse me, sir, when's the next train to Batesville?"

"Same time tomorrow, sir. Nothing 'til then."

"Are there trains from other companies?"

"No, sir, no trains before then. Sorry."

"Thanks." Tam slipped him a quarter.

"Damn!" said David. He composed himself. "At least we know his appearance, that we're on the right track, no pun intended, and that he doesn't have much of a start on us."

"We'll catch him when we get into the wilds of Arkansas." The friends retraced their steps to quiz John Sutherland.

Chapter 10

George had had enough. His sister Bella had been pacing the corridors of their train for days now, which meant that he had had to drop everything and accompany her. But today was the worst. She was parading less but it seemed like every five minutes, she was asking, "What time is it?" or "How long till we get there?"

Stifling a nasty retort, he added aggrieved patience to his tone and told her.

This time, she caught the undercurrent in his response. "George, I'm sorry to keep bothering you, but I'm so anxious to see Ma and Pa again. I've so much to tell them and I can't wait. Do you think they'll have crossed the Bay from San Francisco to Oakland to meet us?"

"It'll depend on whether Da has found a job. Uncle Jack was a woodworker too, you know, and I think he was going to see about getting Da a job in the furniture factory he works for. And if he has found a job, he can't take time off having just started.

And he wouldn't let Ma come all this way by hersel', especially in a strange city. I'm not holding my hopes up that we'll see them until we get to Uncle Jack's house."

He saw Bella's face fall and thought a change of subject was in order. "I've been talking to some blokes in the bar and they tell me San Francisco is booming, which is good news for us job-seekers."

"What kind of work are you going to look for, George?"

George laughed. "Anything that brings in some groceries. I eat a lot, if you hadn't noticed."

Bella punched his arm. "How could I miss that; you're always starving!" She returned to her first topic. "Oh, I hope they're there to meet us."

*   *   *

At last, the train crept into the Oakland station. After the barren plains and the sheer but empty grandeur of the Rockies, the siblings enjoyed re-entering civilization again.

But the happy reunion was not to be. Harry, (Bella and George's Da), had started work that very day with his brother Jack, and their Ma', Fiona, didn't dare venture onto the streets of San Francisco. Other than the few days in Glasgow, this was the only big city she had been in and was fair intimidated by the City's hustle and bustle and its smells and noise and crowds.

Bella scanned the thinning throng one last time, then squared her shoulders and turned to her brother. "All right, no Ma and Pa. What next, George?"

George could see his sister's disappointment but determined to make the best of it. "I agree, sis, it doesn't look like they're here. Now we get a ferry to San Francisco and find Uncle Jack's house. Thank goodness Sir David gave us some money before we parted ways in New York. Here, I've even got a porter to help us with your cabin trunk. Let's go."

Chapter 11

"What happened then?" Fiona balled her hankie into her fist and gave it a good chew. Her face was inches from her daughter's, her eyes searching Bella's. She was looking for clues to the outcome of her daughter's kidnapping to the Lederbeiter clan brothel. Bella sat opposite her ma at the kitchen table; brother George was standing by the pantry eating California oranges, apples and strawberries.

"David showed up with George and Tam and a squad of policemen he had hired. They rescued me before I suffered any real harm."

Fiona noticed her lassie had dropped the honorific 'Sir' before David.

"Are you sure you're all right? They didn't..."

"No, Ma, I've a few scrapes and bruises, but otherwise I'm fine."

George studied her from across the room. *What of your nightmares, lassie? You've had enough of them the last few nights.* He decided to hold his tongue, He'd talk to Ma if Bella showed no signs of improvement.

His sister returned to her narrative. "David encouraged his men to destroy the place so it could never be used again. He found the safe filled with jewelry and cash and distributed most of it to the other women. They'd also been kidnapped and forced to work for the Lederbeiters." Her hand flew to her neck and caressed the pendant David had given her.

"Oh, yes, the others, I'd forgotten there were more. Where did they go?"

"David handed them over to a woman from the Immigrants Aid Society, an actual Society this time, but we women exacted revenge on the Lederbeiters before leaving." Bella managed a weak laugh. "We turned the Lederbeiters out into the streets with no money, no prospects and no clothes other than their unmentionables!"

"In their bloomers?" Even Fiona had to chuckle. "I wish I'd seen that! But I still think the authorities should lock them up in a cellar full of rats and throw the key away!" Fiona's voice rose as she allowed her anger to surface, but her curiosity calmed her.

"Your pendant is beautiful." She reached over and examined it. "Did Sir David give you that?"

"Yes, Ma, he did. He provided money so George and I could get a sleeping cabin, but this was a personal gift to me."

"A personal gift?"

"Yes, Ma, a special gift. It's what two people in love do, give gifts."

"Aaah, in love, you say. But he's ..."

"Nobility. I know, Ma, but they're not all the same. David's exceptional and different and I love him so much." Color came back to her cheeks as she drifted off to dream of her white knight.

"Where is he now? Did he travel with you on the train?"

"No, he had family business in Arkansas. That's a state somewhere in the South. Once he's finished, he'll come and find me."

"Huh! He says!" Fiona grunted in disbelief. "George, what do you make of this Sir David? Is he the same as the others?"

"No, Ma. He seemed to have Bella's best interests at heart."

Fiona was less than pacified.

Chapter 12

The depot on Lawrence Street in Batesville, Arkansas, was a far cry from the great station of St. Louis. It was a single-story affair, seriously lacking in grand ceilings or gilded arches. It was all business, utilitarian, but what it suffered in plainness, it made up for in commerce.

The Thomases dallied as they stepped from their railcar, watching the railway workers on the other track hefting bales of cotton from a six-mule wagon onto a freight train. Flatbeds of oak and hickory, pre-cut into boards, were headed for markets in the north. Most of the stevedores were Negroes, but a few Irish accents swore at the hot sun. It was easy to tell where they got their nickname "redlegs"; their sunburns were spectacular and painful. Relief was in sight, though. A line of thunderstorms was marching towards them, black, looming, evil clouds like medieval cathedrals, spitting fire and brimstone, rumbling like a giant with internal distress.

With practiced ease, the porter slung the Thomases' baggage onto the waiting buckboard. The buckboard's driver was old, shrunken, grizzled and one-legged. He geed his horse into a walk, concentrating on navigating through other traffic until he had left the bustle of the terminal.

"Well, where are you two fancy pants off to, eh?"

Thomas Senior bristled at the coachman's familiarity. "Keep a civil tongue in your head! Where we're going is none of your business!"

"Hey, if you don't like it, I'll let you off here!" The driver grinned, his shortage of teeth making him look like a gargoyle.

"Here" was a rundown section of Batesville near the Poke Bayou, dirty, disreputable and dangerous, populated by drunks and deadbeats. The Thomases felt the derelicts' eyes tracking them, longing and desperation writ large. This was not a place to be marooned.

Thomas Junior reacted instantly. "We're off to Rush. What can you tell us about it?"

"Rush, eh? First off, good luck! You're gonna need it. There's no law and order there. Many people arrived runnin' from justice and old habits die hard.

With your swanky clothes, you'll be a beacon for bandits. Why, it'd surprise me if you manage ten miles without bein' bushwhacked, and you'll never get out alive. You'd better hire yourself a bunch of protection. Rush, you say?"

"Yes, then to the nearest railhead."

"You're in luck. A few of Quantrill's Raiders hang out there. I'd see if they'd go along with you."

Junior was warming to the driver. "What's your name?"

"Randolph, sir, Randolph Washington. And to answer your next question, it got shot off in the war!" Rapping his wooden leg, he said this without bitterness or self-pity. It was what it was.

"The war?"

"Yes, the War of Northern Aggression. Your Yankee friends call it the Civil War."

"I see." Junior didn't, his knowledge of recent American history was non-existent. "Who are the Quant...?"

"Quantrill's Raiders. They's a gang of bushwhackers who forgot to stop fightin' after the war. Their boss, Quantrill, died years past, but a few of his men still raise havoc whenever they can. 'Course, that's seldom nowadays, they're reachin' their sixties like me. But their reputation makes folks give 'em a wide berth." He leaned over the side of the rig and spat onto the back of a startled alley cat.

"Where do we find them?"

"I'd ask the deckhands on the boat. Some Raiders live near Rush and the hands will know where they hang out. Buck Hall's in charge. Be careful, though, he don't take kindly to strangers!"

Randolph drew up at the levee and the Thomases stared in amazement, never having seen a sternwheeler. There were two of them tied up at the riverbank: the *Ozark Queen* and the *Jessie Blair*. The *Queen* was small, 45 paces long and eight wide, as different as night and day from the transatlantic liners which had brought them to America. The wheel itself had ten feet showing above the waterline, but the superstructure dwarfed it. Rising thirty feet above the deck, it housed the engine room and cargo at water level and the passengers in the overhead cabins. Towering another eighteen feet stood two smokestacks, dormant today. However, it was huge beside the *Blair*, which stretched 30 paces at most.

Senior spluttered. "What the hell's this?"

His son tried to soothe him. "This is the *Ozark Queen*. It'll take us to Buffalo City. How long is our trip up river, Randolph?"

"Don't rightly know sir. It depends on the current." He cocked an eye at the thunderclouds. "And the weather."

Right on cue, the first raindrops cratered the earthy dust on the road. Before they could find shelter, the heavens opened, changing the street into a stream and the dust into mud. Randolph pulled a tarpaulin over his head. "I'd get aboard and find a berth. It'll fill up fast, what with the miners flockin' there."

Father and son exchanged glances, and their pulse rate rose a notch. At long last, "their" mine was becoming tangible, concrete, real. It was no longer an insubstantial concept floating by like a will-o'-the-wisp.

Thomas Senior's take-charge attitude returned. "Michael, pick up our luggage and check us in. There are plenty of porters to give you a hand. I'll pay off Mister Washington here." (That's 'Mister' with a sneer. He still harbored a grudge against the driver for threatening to drop them off in the roughest part of town.) Junior engaged a porter who loaded their bags into a handcart and trundled off down the ramp, eager to evade the rain.

Senior turned to Randolph who had stepped from the buckboard. "Are you going to rob me blind? How much do I owe you?"

"One dollar, sir." Randolph ignored the insult and touched a finger to his brow. As usual, when money was being discussed, the hopeful recipient's deference was in proportion to the size of the sum in question.

Thomas pulled out his purse. "You're not worth that, here's a quarter." And he flipped a coin in the air just out of Randolph's reach, spinning it lazily in the gloom of the afternoon, until it dropped into the muck.

Thomas Senior's laughter choked in his throat when a knife appeared in Randolph's hand. Senior's deteriorating mind had him thinking of too many responses, turn, flee, avoid the blade, protest, scream for help. He managed none of that but caught his boots in a tangle, overbalanced and fell on his back, joining his money in the quagmire. He felt the knife-tip pricking his Adam's apple and thought his last day had come.

Randolph's soft whisper sounded even more menacing. "I could carve you up like a turkey and nobody here'd bat an eyelid, Mr. Fancy Pants. Give me your purse."

Thomas scrabbled through the sludge to find it. "Here! Take it! Take everything!" He propped himself up on his hands.

Randolph shook the coins into his palm. "No, I'll take what I'm due." He held up a silver dollar. "And somethin' for my trouble!" He picked out four quarters. "Mr. Fancy Pants, you're a lucky man." Randolph knelt closer and spoke softer. Thomas smelled the whiskey on his breath. "If you try your little trick with Buck Hall's boys, they'll slice you like a Christmas goose." Randolph stood up, balanced on his good limb, and used his peg leg to push Thomas back into the mire. "I'd pay money to see that."

Chapter 13

Thomas Senior rushed down the stage to the *Ozark Queen*, babbling. "Michael, where are you? Where are you?"

"Right here, Da. What's the matter? Have you spotted Rennie again?" Junior scanned the levee.

"No, it was the coachman, Washington. He tried to kill me!" Thomas's recollection of events was changing so that he would come out smelling like a rose, a tough accomplishment with the mud and manure of the wharf staining his clothes. He gave his sanitized version of the interplay between him and Washington, how Washington had pulled a knife and demanded his purse and how he had fought him off single-handed. Meanwhile, Thomas was scanning the gangplank to check whether Washington was coming after him. No, no sign of him. Thomas relaxed.

"I need to change, where's our cabin?"

"On the deck above, number three."

"When do we leave this godforsaken pimple and what time is dinner?"

"We get underway at daybreak and will be on board for three nights, if the weather holds. Dinner's in an hour. I've seen the menu and I'm impressed. We'll dine well. Oh, and afterwards, there's gambling."

"Huh, I'll believe we'll eat well when I taste it. Your judgment is pathetic when it comes to food!"

Thomas Junior colored from the slight. Again he looked forward to stealing the satchel and scarpering.

The interchange had not gone unnoticed by their 20 fellow passengers, half of whom were professional card sharks. *A house divided is a house conquered.* Conflict between players was invariably good for business.

The meal more than lived up to Michael's promise. Smartly dressed stewards served it in the elegant parlor, a small but comfortable space with oak paneling and deep green carpets. Dining tables occupied the center of the room and easy chairs flanked the glass-topped tables around the perimeter. These sported kerosene lamps and a variety of the latest newspapers and periodicals. To his surprise, Senior enjoyed his meal of seafood chowder, freshwater oysters, a huge, succulent peppercorn steak, and peach cobbler. The wine list also excited him, and he drank far more than he should, growing more and more garrulous, slurring his words, spilling his drink, even loosening his tie.

Once the diners finished their meal, the wait staff cleared the tables and set them up for poker.

"Would you care to join us in a game of cards, suh?" a card player asked Senior. This was Johnny Q, a renowned Mississippi gambler. He looked like one too: muscular, menacing and bald as a billiard ball, wearing smoky glasses and dark shirts and pants. Often, he'd won against inferior opponents by intimidation alone. But Senior declined. It had been a long day, and gambling required a fresh brain.

"Not tonight, thank you." he slurred, "Maybe tomorrow. In fact, tomorrow for sure."

Chapter 14

At dawn, the Ozark *Queen* stumbled into life. Deckhands loaded the final goods using the hoists which required them to bellow at each other. The heavy rain had continued overnight and the pounding on the roof was also a serious irritant to Thomas Senior's hangover. He declined the promised breakfast, but Junior dined well on a shrimp omelet, beignets and chicory coffee.

Before he'd finished his meal, two of last night's gamblers, Johnny Q and Duke, approached. "Where's your father?" No pleasantries here. This was business... serious business.

"Sleeping it off as usual. He won't appear until much later." Junior had lots of experience propping up his father's latest story.

"He's like this every day?" (Translation: Will he be drunk this evening?)

"I'd say so, he enjoys his brandy."

The atmosphere thawed a little. "We look forward to seeing him after dinner. Please send him our regards."

As the sternwheeler churned upstream, Senior kept to the cabin. Junior spent his time talking to an old miner who had been to San Francisco on the way to the California gold fields back in '45. They drank somewhat, but Junior stopped before dusk settled on the river. He needed to be alert if he was to secure "his" money in the satchel. Oh, yes, and to protect his parent. The boat arrived in Buffalo City and tied down. The crew found cords of hot pine cut by the locals and loaded them onto the *Queen* while the travelers enjoyed a delicious dinner of rack of lamb with baby carrots preceded by more freshwater oysters.

"Where do these oysters come from? They're superb!" Senior waved his fork around, spraying dipping sauce over everyone close. He was in his "drunken idiot" persona.

"Why, heah, suh, heah on the White River. Mebbe you noticed people on the mudflats with long rakes an' wickah baskets?" the steward asked.

"I wondered what they were doing. Harvesting oysters, you say?"

"Yes suh, oysters for eatin' and sellin' to the boats. They's also huntin' for pearls, beggin' y'all's pahdon, suh."

"Pearls?! I don't believe you!"

"Oh, that's true, Mr. Thomas, they got pearls in them a'right." This was Johnny Q. "Look." He turned his face so the Thomases could examine the luminous pearl in his left ear. "This stud was found in this very river. I bought it at Bee's Landing for $2."

The Englishmen had never seen such a thing, not merely a man with an earring but the pearl was large and beautiful and, if they could believe Johnny Q, cheap.

"We need to buy a bucketful of these and take them with us. We'd make a fortune!"

Junior agreed, but only after he had the bearer bonds in his grasp. He'd buy the best pearls for himself and sell them in San Francisco.

The cognac was poured and the cigars lit. Senior had polished of two bottles of wine over dinner and appeared drunker than the previous night. The vultures circled.

"Poker?" asked Thomas Senior. "I've heard of poker. How do you play?"

The card sharks had a tough time containing their delight: a drunken pigeon with more money than sense. They took great pains to explain the rules, but omitted the strategic aspects of the game.

"Why not play a few hands while I watch?" Senior slurred, continuing his assault on a fine bottle of VSOP cognac. Junior stood behind him, knowing what was about to happen.

Thirty minutes later, Senior asked to join in, bet small, won small, got 'drunker', then wagered larger, lost a few, won a few, courtesy of the gamblers who were priming him for to lose big. Even Junior spotted their cheating and signaling. Just as Johnny Q and his gang were about to execute the coup, Senior burped, put his forearms on the table, dropped his head to his arms and went to sleep!

"What the hell!"

"He can't go to sleep!"

"Wake him!" This from the leading gambler, Johnny Q.

But no matter how much poking, prodding or dousing Senior endured, they couldn't rouse him. Junior gave the other gamblers the bad news. "Gentlemen, he's out and won't recover until tomorrow. But I guarantee he'll want to play again; he's enjoyed himself. Thanks for letting him join your game. We'll be here in the evening." Junior gathered up Senior's winnings and, with the help of a steward, walked his father back to his room.

The sharks weren't happy with this turn of events, but what could they do? You can't force an unconscious man to play. They grumbled and complained, but left satisfied, having extracted a promise from Junior that his father would show up the next evening.

Once father and son reached the safety of their cabin, Senior opened an eye, confirmed that they were alone, sat up and grinned at his son. Gone was the slurring, the staggering and the stupidity; his mind was clear as a bell. He had started drinking in earnest when he was eleven years old, so a carafe of wine and a few brandies made no impression on him.

"This'll be fun, Michael! Did you see how they were setting me up for a beating? And their signals between themselves? Why didn't they use semaphore flags! A bunch of amateurs! Except for Johnny Q. I couldn't pick up any of his tells."

"You did well, Da. But don't underestimate them; they're a rough lot. Did you spot the guns and knives they had? I think they'd use 'em without a second thought. Be careful!"

Chapter 15

While the Thomases were churning up the White River, the Scots were stepping down from their train's third-class carriage in Batesville. The five-hour journey from St. Louis had been less comfortable than their first-class meanderings of late, the wooden slats leaving imprints on their bums. They had trimmed their luggage to a bag each and were wearing their new old clothing. David's beard was beginning to look as though he meant it, while Tam was his usual dashing self, whiskers curling, eyes seeking mischief. Each of them had a pistol with plenty of ammunition.

Two buckboards worked the train depot, so hiring Randolph Washington wasn't much of a coincidence. They climbed aboard, David sitting beside the driver, Tam in the rear.

"Where to, gents?"

"The docks, we're looking for a steamer to Rush."

"You too, eh? Say, ain't you got a fancy foreign accent? Are you kin to those swells from yesterday?" Randolph's voice hardened, his memory of yesterday's 'swells' fresh and foul.

"You mean you saw the Thomases?" Tam leant forward from the back seat, unable to restrain himself or to hide his excitement. "Two men, one around 50, short, fat, well-dressed, clutching a satchel, the other his son, twenties. Don't know what he looks like. Is that them?"

"Yep, that be them awright. Why, friends of your'n?" Again, suspicion colored Randolph's tone.

"Hell, no! Quite the opposite. They're thieves and crooks. Where did you take them?"

Tam's obvious dislike for the Senior and Junior relaxed Randolph. "Same as you, they were looking for a boat to Rush." He paused. "Dadgummit! I gave them Buck Hall's name to buy themselves protection. They sure don't deserve that!"

"Who's Buck Hall, why the need for protection, and why don't they deserve it, sir?"

The driver told the Scots of the Raiders, the dangers facing travelers in Arkansas, and how Thomas Senior had treated him.

"That's Thomas right enough. He can't tell you the color of the sun without lying or swindling money out of it." David growled.

"You're chasing him because…?" Randolph let the question hang.

Tam deferred to his protege, who hesitated. Scots were a reticent lot and didn't broadcast their private affairs. But David liked the openness he had enjoyed in America and considered he had more to gain than lose. "He cheated my father and his business acquaintances out of a considerable amount of money. I'm here to retrieve it." His voice sounded like cold steel. Even Randolph flinched.

"I may have done harm to y'all." The driver managed to look contrite. "Before the old man tried to screw me out of my fare, I told him to hire Buck and his boys to protect them, otherwise they'd not live long. Fancy Pants! Huh!" Randolph's disgust with himself was clear. He explained Hall's background with Quantrill's bushwhackers. "Things'll get real nasty if you tangle with them, but if you come 'cross them, say 'Debris' and tell them I sent you!"

"'Debris!' Why is 'Debris' so special?"

"It's a code word around Quantrill's boys. It'll make sure Buck hears you out afore he shoots you!"

The Scots digested this unpleasant news.

"How do you know so much about Quantrill's gang?" asked Tam.

"I used to ride with 'em years back. No longer, though."

"Why not, if you don't mind me asking?"

"'Cause I found the Lord!"

Talk about a conversation stopper. *How do you respond to that?* thought David. The awkwardness passed when Randolph inquired, "Why is Rush so all-fired important, you folks showing up in droves 'n'all?"

"The ownership of a mine's in dispute. We need to go to the Land Office there to confirm our title before Thomas bribes someone."

Randolph considered this for a moment, then chuckled, then laughed, then roared. He had to stop the buckboard before he lost control of it.

"What did I say?"

Their driver spluttered for another minute, then steadied himself. "It isn't what you said, sir. It's how the good Lord looks after his own."

"I don't understand." David was still unamused.

"This Thomas fella is off to the Rush Land Office, eh?"

"Yes, I expect so!"

Randolph laughed harder. "He's gonna be surprised!"

"How so?"

"There's one Land Office in Northwest Arkansas. Guess where. I'll give you a hint: it's not in Rush!"

"It's not? I assumed it would be. Where is it then?"

"Right here in Batesville! And they missed it!"

Once again, Randolph stopped the conversation in its tracks.

Chapter 16

David asked their driver to change their destination, and they pulled up outside the State Land Office in minutes. "Randolph, wait for us. This should take care of your time." The young noble pushed a bundle of notes into the driver's open hand.

Washington glanced at the bills and saw all was good, very good.

"Yes sir! I'll stay here until tomorrow if need be!"

David retrieved the mine's ownership papers from his baggage, entered the Land Office with Tam at his heels and sought out the manager.

Levoy Broderick was a precise man, an ideal attribute for the person holding one of the more important positions in Arkansas. He groomed himself with care, sporting a black worsted wool suit with a mustard-colored vest. His white shirt and starched collar were immaculate, and his muted red necktie was kept in place by a gold stickpin. A matching set of pince-nez glasses perched on the end of his pudgy nose. He had parted the remains of his hair in the middle and dyed it an unnatural shade of brown.

His office was also orderly. Hardwood bookcases held row upon row of ledgers, marked and filed in alphabetical order. His desk, free of the usual clutter, was on a riser and the chairs in front of it cut low, so he'd look down on his clients while they peered up at him. No doubt he felt he needed this stage management because he was short of five feet tall and sensitive to commanding respect. Nevertheless, what he lacked in stature, he made up in intellect.

He quickly grasped David's intention, settled the pince-nez and examined the documents David had brought. He inspected the transfer of the mine's ownership from Lord Rennie to his son, rising to check the title deed against his huge register of lands, minerals and mines. "Everything's in order except for the annual maintenance fee. That'll be ten dollars." His voice was a high tenor.

The Scots smiled at each other, recognizing the scam, but David was happy to pay the extortion. If that's what it took to confirm ownership, it was cheap at twice the price.

"Of course. Here you are, sir. Please write a receipt and a certified letter from you confirming my takeover, if you don't mind." Honey and money works wonders.

The civil servant whistled through his mustache. It was a grand, bushy affair also designed to increase his credibility. "We don't provide letters as a rule, most irregular, I'd say, most irregular."

Where had David heard that before! "I expect to compensate you, Mr. Broderick. Will this do?"

Money changed hands. Not enough. More. "This is acceptable, thank you." The land manager began to write."Here you are, signed and sealed. Funny you should show up today."

"How so?"

"This is the second enquiry into the Evening Star I've had this week."

"What? Who else was asking? A round, stocky fellow with an English accent?" David fumed at the thought of Randolph misleading him.

"No, it was Stanley Chase from the Morning Star mine. He's a lanky beanpole, must be someone different than you have in mind."

The young Scot relaxed. "Where's the Morning Star?"

Broderick smiled. "It's your neighbor in Rush, the highest-producing property around here!"

David tried to hide his excitement.

Broderick continued. "It sounded as though he was interested in buying your mine, seeing as you're adjacent an' all."

"Is that so? Stanley Chase, you say. Is he here in Batesville?"

"Nah, he sailed for Rush earlier today on the *Ozark Queen*. Why? Do you want to sell?"

"I doubt it." *Whatever I tell Broderick, the whole world will know within hours. Keep my thoughts to myself.*

*　　*　　*

And the endgame started, with an idea and the beginning of a plan.

Chapter 17

*B*ella, my dearie.

David was sitting with his back against a tree on the banks of the White River, waiting for the crew to load the sternwheeler with wood for the hungry boilers. He started his letter once again. His earlier efforts were too formal or too familiar or too disconnected from the feeling he had for his love. He decided to write what was in his heart and damn the prose and propriety.

I cannot believe so few days have passed since we were in each other's arms. It's as though eternity and immeasurable distance have grown between us, and I yearn for it not to be so. I remember saying when we had breakfast aboard the SS Curambria I couldn't fathom the workings of the fate that threw our lives together. Despite the horrible circumstances, I am forever grateful because my life purpose is now set. I mean to find you and never let you go. I must finish my task here in Arkansas before I come for you, but I am making progress.

David described bumping into Thomas in St. Louis, then continued:

> *Tam and I are on board a wee steamer called the Jessie Blair heading up a tributary of the mighty Mississippi. It's a sternwheeler, which means a massive paddlewheel at the back propels it through the currents and shoals of this treacherous river. This wheel allows it to navigate in very shallow water; one of our companions said it only needed a heavy dew! Times, the craft gets stuck anyway and the deckhands tie thick ropes round trees and use capstans, a pulley system, to haul the boat past the obstruction. We passengers take turns in pushing on the capstan's bars, no standing on the sidelines here, pulling rank. We're treated as equals; I love that about America!*

> *I fear you might change your feelings for me if you saw me now. Tam and I are traveling in steerage class with the miners and I'm dressed as one in a ratty old work shirt, hob-nailed boots and trousers made*

from a tough cloth called denim. I'm lucky, my denims are well-washed so they're as soft as a baby's bum, but Tam's are newer and he's chafing and complaining. All this is to enable us to fit in with our travel companions for our own safety. I won't gloss over the dangers we face. This is a desperate part of the world but we're fully provisioned and alert to our surroundings and I have Tam to deter anyone who has hostile thoughts.

Arkansas is a conundrum. It's beautiful and backward and flat and hilly. When we first came aboard, a white swathe of cotton fields surrounded us but later we headed into the hills. We are now in a rugged glen with hundred-foot cliffs on either side, clothed in virgin stands of oak.

Arkansas resembles Scotland with burns, called creeks here, and hills and forests. The fall foliage is putting on an impressive display for us. Imagine an autumn back home and multiply by ten! Our normal autumn colors are visible, but more so. The golds are richer, the reds are deeper and more vivid. Yellow aspens resemble our birch trees, but, again, more *so. It's a magnificent sight, and I wish you were here to share it with me.*

The waters are clear and filled with fish. At one tough spot where we had to manhandle the steamer over a shoal, a boy took his fishing rod and pulled in dozens of trout in a few scant hours. There are lots of game, deer to be sure, but bigger animals too, elk, they're called. I'm told bears roam the woods, wild cats too.

But the biggest danger comes from the two-legged beasties. Lawlessness is a common way of life here, so we keep our foreign voices low and our profile lower, nothing to draw attention to ourselves. We land at Buffalo City tomorrow, then make our way to Rush, where I hope to confront Thomas and take ownership of the mine.

But what of you, my love? How was your journey from New York? I trust it was comfortable and uneventful. By the time this letter reaches you, you'll be well-settled into San Francisco. What kind of place is it? I know little of it. It's a seaport, and will have a rough edge, I'm sure. But it's the major city on the west side of America so I'd expect a posh district too, which augurs well for finding a tutoring job, should you so desire. Oh, my dear, what a country! Life is so full of possibilities. I just wish we were together to grasp them.

I'll leave you now and ready this for posting tomorrow. Please know I go to sleep with your beautiful face in mind, your lips on my lips, your hand in my hand. Until this is a reality, think of me often with warm and tender thoughts, as I will think of you.

Until you're in my arms again,

All my love,
David.

Chapter 18

Five players gathered to battle with Thomas Senior. The four opponents from the earlier evening, Johnny Q, Duke and their two accomplices, licked their chops anticipating the drubbing they planned on giving him. The unknown fifth player had watched from the sidelines the night before. He looked for all the world like an apocalyptic undertaker: older, tall, thin, his dense black beard shot with gray under a black homburg and over a black suit. He wasn't here to socialize but to gamble, which he did successfully. Johnny Q even sought to distract him at one point by bringing in Serafina, his most curvaceous girl. The Undertaker, showing spectacular concentration, ignored her.

The first few hands resembled the prior nights. Senior won a few and lost more while the sharks positioned themselves for a major fleecing. The Undertaker was a wild card, building a nice stack of chips for himself.

Thomas had been drinking copious amounts of brandy and appeared drunker than the previous night. He delighted the professional gamblers when he slurred, "Must we have a limit on how much we bet? I want to recoup my losses!"

Johnny Q tried to hide his glee. "No, sah, we don't have to have no maximum. We can play 'No Limit' unless anyone objects." His cronies agreed, feigning reluctance.

Thomas asked. "What does 'No Limit' mean?"

The gambler explained, and Thomas, stumbling over his words, approved.

The competitors turned to the man in black who fixed Thomas with a gaze so piercing that even he, the most brazen of liars, became uncomfortable.

The Undertaker nodded, "Yes, I'm in." That was all he said until the conclusion of his evening.

The intensity of the poker picked up with less chatter, more focus, more cheating, more signaling by Johnny Q and his pals. But Thomas, despite appearing drunk, smelled out every trap and threw in when he was about to lose large, and bid big when he had the best cards. Soon, he had a decent stake in front of him, as did Johnny Q, who scored at the expense of his colleagues. The black-suited newcomer, who followed Thomas's style of play, amassed a substantial pile of winnings of his own.

Spectators lined the walls of the saloon where the cigar smoke lay thick and heavy. Junior stood behind his Da to stop the most blatant duplicity, a shill peering at Senior's cards over his shoulder, for example.

At the end of the second hour, Duke, Johnny Q's henchman, had a surge of idiocy and went all in, sure his full house was the top hand. Everyone folded except Thomas who inquired, "Do four twos beat a full house?"

The Duke's eyes bugged out of his head. He watched dumfounded as Thomas laid his deuces on the table, one at a time, crowing as he did so. Nobody ever accused him of being a gracious winner! His adversaries stared at him long and hard, adjusting their original opinions of Thomas.

Thirty minutes later, The Undertaker took out a Johnny Q flunky, his flush beating the crony's straight. Johnny Q gave The Undertaker a reappraising stare. A mind reader might have seen Johnny Q figure Thomas for no rookie, and no sot either, and the older man to be a daunting opponent in his own right. Heaven forbid if they were in cahoots and playing together! He figured he needed as many chips as possible to survive and win, so he set up and cleaned out his final crony, to this accomplice's considerable disgust.

The dealer called a comfort break, but the Undertaker shocked his rivals when he announced, "Thank you for the game, gentlemen. I'd love to continue, but I need my sleep. Good night!"

"Now wait a minute, fellah! Where do you think you're going with my money?" The gambler's aggressive tone didn't bode well for the Undertaker. But six miners stepped forward from the shadows, each holding a gun. They outnumbered Johnny Q's men, who eased their mitts away from their pistol butts.

"If you recall, I took little from you. It was these unfortunate gentlemen who had a poor evening." He tipped his hat to Johnny Q's followers and rose from his chair, leaving consternation in his wake.

Chapter 19

Thomas knocked his chair over, trying to catch up with the Undertaker, telling Junior to guard his money. "Sir! Sir! May I have a word?" No drunkenness now, his façade had slipped.

The Undertaker had reached the deck but stopped as Senior emerged from the parlor. He nodded and two of the accompanying miners grabbed Senior's arms and held tight,

Thomas recovered his composure. "My apologies, sir, my apologies, I didn't mean to startle you." He glared at the men holding him, but they kept their grip. "May I ask your name, sir?"

"Chase. Stanley Chase." He was as economical with words as he was with movement.

"Mr. Chase, let me congratulate you on a game well played? Commendable, highly commendable. And your exit! Did you see Johnny Q's face when you stood up to leave? He near to had a heart attack! And he had murder in his eyes, I'll tell you that for nothing!" Senior was babbling; Chase's lack of response was agitating him. He jabbered on. "You're right to have your boys stationed round the room, we're playing with a rough lot. A rough lot indeed. Calls for as much protection as you can get, doesn't it?"

Once again, no response from Chase.

"It's your boys I need to discuss. I want to hire them for my own safety. I'll need them if I beat Johnny Q head-to-head." Thomas tried an ingratiating smile, but it came out crooked and desperate.

Chase continued to stare at him, unnerving Thomas anew. At last, Chase spoke. "Who are you?"

For a moment, Senior couldn't remember which part he was performing but settled on Russian nobility. "Tookov, sir, Baron Pyotr Tookov at your service." His accent changed to match the new persona.

Chase noticed the rebirth. Another long penetrating pause. "And what's your business here, Baron Tookov?"

"I own a mine called the Evening Star in Rush."

Chase actually blinked. An even longer hesitation this time. He signed to his men, who released Thomas. "Melvin and Pete will go with you and keep you safe. We'll take breakfast in the morning, nine o'clock. Goodnight, Baron."

Was there a slight emphasis on "Baron", a measure of disbelief?

Chapter 20

A Johnny Q flunky came searching for Thomas. "Ah, there you be! Are you ready?"

Thomas cloaked himself in his stumbling drunk persona and returned to the saloon. "You and me, Johnny Q, you and me. I'm looking forward to our duel. I'll learn a lot from you."

The gambler had no illusions as to Senior's gambling prowess, but played along.

Thomas continued, "I have a request. I want to play with a different pack of cards. The other players may have marked these and I'd prefer we started fresh."

Johnny Q hesitated, figured he could mark the new deck just as quickly as Thomas, and nodded in agreement.

"Oh, another thing. Is there a shoe available?"

This gave the card shark pause. "A shoe, Sah, a shoe? Why do we need a shoe?"

"Our dealer here," Thomas acknowledged the chief steward, Henri, who was pulling double duty, "deals off the bottom. If he has to deal from a shoe, he won't be able to affect the outcome of our game."

Henri glanced towards Johnny Q and back to his accuser. He didn't protest... guilty as charged. He wondered whether he'd see the bribe money he'd been promised.

The master gambler took a pull on his whiskey. "You're not as stupid as you look, are you? Or as pickled. Aw'right, a clean deck and a shoe." The dealer hustled off to find both.

Thomas ignored the insults and settled in for a protracted night of poker. He saw Melvin, Pete, and two other miners from Chase's crew return and position themselves along the walls of the game room. Thomas acknowledged them with a wave, figuring there was no harm in letting his opponent know he had protection.

Junior stationed himself behind Senior's chair, grasping the leather satchel tight to his waistcoat. No emotion appeared on his face: he'd have made an excellent poker player himself. But inside, his guts churned and bile erupted in his throat from the stress of trying to figure out how the evening might end. If his father lost, all would be well. The other, and probable, scenario had Senior beat Johnny Q resulting in blood being spilled. His father was a poor winner. *It's not going to be my blood, nor am I going to lose these bearer bonds.*

He clutched the satchel to his bosom like a woman with her newborn. He slipped out unnoticed while the gamblers fussed over Henri's missteps. He collected the newspapers scattered on the side tables and came back to the game minutes later, still clutching the satchel.

The action was intense. Senior had stopped drinking and dropped the rookie player mask and was all business. He portrayed a ruthless focus, chewing on an unlit cheroot which he tongued from one side of his mouth to the other. The professional gambler was no less absorbed, eyes hooded, hands hooded, watching Thomas and Henri like a hawk at supper time. The dealer was behaving himself. He had no choice, he had to use the shoe. Thomas and Johnny Q, however, compensated for his righteousness, their fingernails hard at work marking the cards.

The competition between the pair sawed back and forth. First Johnny Q faced disaster, but an infusion of cash from an inside pocket staved off defeat and kept him alive. Then it was Thomas's turn to teeter on the edge of ruin, but a rare ill-advised call by Johnny Q of his opponent's full house jumped him into the lead.

The audience were seeing masterful performances by actors at the peak of their game. The end, when it happened, was almost anti-climactic.

The card shark lagged in chips but picked up a good hand: three kings. His second draw card, also a king, made it great! He could see precious little of his opponent's cards, but his own fingernail marks suggested Thomas held a mixed hand, useful only for bluffing. Johnny Q played it slow. Thomas was cautious too, but each round of bidding mounted until it was obvious to the onlookers that both of the combatants had exceptional cards, or else a monumental bluff was being attempted. Thomas dithered over his final bet.

"All in!"

"I call!"

The buzz around the room grew, then subsided to a deafening hush. This was it, the finale of two classic nights of high caliber poker.

Johnny Q laid his four kings on the baize table-cloth, imitating Thomas's crowing, his gang whooping in support. He reached to scoop up the pot.

"Not so fast, Johnny Q. Not so fast." Thomas placed his cards on the table one at a time, low cards to be sure but in order and all the same suit. A straight flush!

Now who was doing the crowing! Thomas leaped from his seat and danced a jig, his left hand on his hip, the right over his head, forefinger wagging to the beat of his own drummer.

Johnny Q couldn't believe his eyes. He snatched up the winning hand and examined the markings, fury erupting from every fiber of his being. "What the hell...? You cheatin' son-of-a-gun! You rogued me! You switched my markings!" The irony of who cheated whom first escaped him. "You drunken old sot, you'll never get away with this!" He scanned the lounge for his cronies to correct this grievous wrong then realized Mr. Chase's men had stepped forward and were covering him and his flunkies with their pistols.

Senior laughed and rubbed salt in the gambler's wounds. "What a bunch of amateurs! Why, my grandmother could whip you and she's blind." Thomas gathered up his winnings, shoveled the greasy bills into the satchel and strode off to his cabin with his son, while the miners covered his exit.

Junior didn't think they'd live through the night.

Chapter 21

Thomas Senior slept the sleep of the just, but his son, Michael Junior, not for a minute. The young man stressed and fretted and tossed and turned, worrying himself awake long after the blackest hours of night had passed.

When should I disappear with the bonds and the poker winnings? Should I wait to see if Da can squeeze money out of the mine? He says it could be worth thousands upon thousands of dollars. Where would I go? San Francisco sounds promising, but how do I get there? Catch a train, I suppose, but where's the nearest railhead? Why am I fretting about San Francisco? If Johnny Q. has his way, we won't live to enjoy daylight!

Doubts and decisions continued to hammer away at him until his overloaded brain felt like exploding. Michael took comfort in knowing Chase had sent two of his miners to cover their door, although their chattering helped keep him from his much-needed sleep.

"What are you thinkin', Melvin? Are we wastin' our time out here or what? I dunno why Mr. Chase is botherin'. This old guy's a right bloody crook, if you ask me."

"He didn' ask you, did he, Pete? The boss's gotta have an excellent reason to protect this geezer, or why pay us extra to stand guard? I agree with you on one thang, though, he's a villain if ever there was. All charm and smile and sticking a blade in yer back when you let yer defenses slip. I would'n' trust him as far as I could throw him!"

Melvin snickered. "That would'n' be far, now would it! You're way too skinny to heave anybody a distance!" They both had a chuckle.

Junior tried to put faces to the sounds and thought he recognized Pete, a skinny runt of a man, but Melvin was an unknown. *Melvin had better be bigger than his mate or I've no chance of surviving.* Michael climbed down from his upper bunk again and paced the well-worn path on his cabin floor while Senior snored on like the Montauk Point foghorn.

Close to three in the morning, fellow miners relieved Pete and Melvin. "Jethro! 'Bout time ya' pulled your head out of your cot!"

"Screw you, Pete. I was right out, dreaming of that wee redhead we met in Batesville. The moment things got interestin', Bubba here had to wake me!"

A new, deep, big voice replied. "I'd have woken you anyhow, our shift or not. You was snorin' fit to wake the graveyard and no one else enjoyed any shuteye. Your dreams were over, man!"

Jethro laughed with the others, then the conversation turned serious. "Anythin' happenin', Pete?"

"Nah, nothin' much, Bubba, although we had company checkin' on us, mebbe an hour ago, would you say, Melvin?"

"Yeah, a drunk comin' by and peein' over the side. But he was more sober than he made out."

"OK, we'll keep our eyes peeled." The big voice took charge. "Hope they tries sumphin'. If Ah'm out of bed, I might as well get mah exercise!" Laughter ensued.

Junior checked the chair he had wedged under the door handle.

At daybreak, the sleepless Michael picked up more chatter. Two of Johnny Q's cohorts had joined the miners on the upper deck.

"Bubba, how come yer guardin' this piece of white trash? You've no dog in this fight."

"No, Seedy, but Mr. Chase does, and he signs mah wage chits."

Junior heard a rumble, a shout, and a splash. It appeared Bubba was a man of action and Seedy had left the boat. Visiting hours were over.

Chapter 22

Thomas Senior woke before eight o'clock and prepared for his meeting with Chase. "Come with me to the saloon, Michael, but sit at a different table, one where you can watch the room. Take the valise and keep it close, you hear? Don't let it out of your grasp!"

Stanley Chase was waiting for them, still dressed in black, still economical in movement and speech. Johnny Q sat strategically between the entrance and Chase. He stood up, grabbed Senior by the arm and hissed in his ear. "I'm gonna get mah money back from you one way or 'nother. Make no mistake. One way or 'nother."

Thomas shook him off and continued to his seat, appearing nonchalant. Only Junior noticed his steps had shortened and accelerated. The gambler had flustered him.

Johnny Q saw Michael at a separate table, clutching the valise. *Mmmh, wonder what's so all-*

fired important for his son to keep such a tight eye on the satchel? Mebbe that's where ma money is.

Chase and Thomas Senior made small talk while enjoying an excellent breakfast: bacon, grits, biscuits and preserves, followed by strong, bitter chicory coffee. They discussed last night's game, ignoring the glowering glares sent their way by Johnny Q and gang. Their waiter cleared the dishes, and they settled down to business.

"Baron Tookov, you're an international man-about-town. How did you come to be the proprietor of a mine in Arkansas? Please, satisfy my curiosity." Southern charm at its smoothest.

"I won it in a card game in London from a British nobleman, Lord Rennie." Thomas/Tookov assumed Chase had done his homework and was familiar with the name of the most recent owner. "I'm here in Arkansas to wrap up the ownership change. What's your interest, Mr. Chase?"

Chase ignored the question. "You haven't conveyed the title, Baron?"

"No, my son and I are off to the Land Office in Rush to complete the transfer."

"To the Rush Land Office, eh? You've been in touch with them?" The miner's voice was getting more subdued as if to counterpoint Thomas/Tookov's bluster.

"Of course. We've corresponded regularly since I won the property. Thought I'd see for myself. find out whether I should work it or sell it. Are you in the mining business, Mr. Chase?"

Once more, no response. Chase's eyes left Thomas, much to his relief; the dead-fish stare unnerved him. It looked as though Chase was playing poker again, calculating odds, adding up possibilities, sorting fact from fiction.

Was this Tookov trustworthy? Not in the least, based on his cheatin' last night and lyin' about his communications in the Land Office. He should have known it was in Batesville. Is he the true owner of the Evening Star? Probably not, for the same reasons. Does it matter? No. If Tookov can show legal ownership after some sleight of hand with Broderick at the Land Office, I'd be interested in buyin' it.

"Baron, I'm aware of an investor who may have an interest in your mine. Before he starts dickerin' with you, though, he'll need to see a proper title transfer. An ironclad title, you know what I mean? What are you askin' for it, anyways?"

Chase's curiosity delighted Thomas/Tookov but being the master poker player, he hid his excitement. It was obvious the "investor" was Chase himself. Asking the selling price was a dead giveaway.

"I'll have a better understanding once I've talked to the Land Office. We dock in Rush soon, don't we? Where will I find you?"

"Ask for me at the Morning Star Hotel; they'll know where I am." Of course they would. Chase was the major shareholder in both the inn and the mine. The mine owner rose from the table and took a step towards the door, then turned back. "Oh, and it might take you longer to transfer the title. The Land Office is in Batesville. Goodbye, Baron, I look forward to meetin' you in Rush...sometime." He walked out on a stunned Tookov.

Chapter 23

Rush was the highest navigable port on the Buffalo River, a center for cotton and timber shipments. It was also the principal embarkation port for ore from the mines in the surrounding hills. Riverboats and barges were constant and noisy visitors with the commotion starting before the sternwheelers negotiated the final bend. Three short piercing blasts from the boat's whistle set off a frenzy of activity, both on board and on the waterfront. Even Thomas Senior sprang into life, despite the depression caused by Chase's closing comment of last night.

'Michael, we have to leave the boat surrounded by as many passengers as possible. Johnny Q won't dare attack us in full view of the townsfolk. Did you find out where Quantrill's Raiders hang out?"

"Yes, Da, at Sweaty Betty's pool room."

"A pool room? Why a pool room? And who's Sweaty Betty?"

"They don't have bars here. This county is dry, but pool rooms fill the void. Sweaty Betty's the owner. Look. There. On the far side of the road."

Thomas gasped. "It's a tent!"

He had a hard time reading the sloppy lettering painted on the shingle, which dangled above the entrance. Wedged between a single story wooden dry goods store and a more substantial two-story stone building, identified as a furniture and coffin maker, the pool room looked pathetic. Business must be good, however, judging by the trail of tracks beating a path to the tent flap that served as a door.

Senior swallowed hard. "Michael, hire a steward to take our baggage to Sweaty Betty's. You and I will have to run the gauntlet from this bucket of rust to her tent." He peeked over his shoulder and sure enough, spotted the gambler and his entourage keeping an evil eye on them. "I really hope Buck Hall is in there."

The *Ozark Queen* tied up and dropped its ramp. First off was Stanley Chase and his retinue, which left the Thomases feeling even more vulnerable. Jostling his way to the front of the queue and still clutching the satchel to his chest, Senior scuttled down the gangway and across the muddy road. Johnny Q and company scrambled to disembark, but a recalcitrant mule delayed them. Johnny Q's oaths were colorful and inventive.

Sweaty Betty's was darker than expected. The strong midday sun had trouble penetrating the layers of grime covering the now-gray tent. It had been "liberated" from the Civil War and had enjoyed many reincarnations. Of the seven men inside, four stood around a pool table that had seen many better days and nights. From the door, the Thomases noted the holes in the baize cloth and how the table listed to the west. Another two occupants sat near the rear of the room watching everyone and everything. These six silently eyed the newcomers. The seventh man slouched over his glass at the bar, singing to himself, drunk as a sailor on his last night of shore leave.

"Can any of you gentlemen direct me to Buck Hall?" Thomas tried to keep the urgency out of his voice.

"Who wants to know?" This from a deep bass, one of the duo lounging in the back.

"Randolph Washington over in Batesville suggested Mister Hall might help me."

There were sniggers from the non-speaking five, the youngest even daring to mimic Senior. "Mister

Hall...!" but the bass, Buck Hall, current leader of Quantrill's Raiders, silenced him with a glare.

"And why do you need his aid?" Buck played it cagey.

As if on cue, Johnny Q and three of his boys burst in, pistols to the fore. Thomas Senior dived for cover beneath the table. Buck Hall rose from his chair. His followers dropped their pool cues, drew their weapons, and covered the outsiders.

The gambler skidded to a halt; he hadn't expected to be outgunned.

"Who the hell are you?" Hall's deep voice was still in command.

Johnny Q blustered and swaggered, struggling to recover the dominant role, but the Raider kept firm. "I say agin, who the hell are you, stranger, and what do you mean burstin' into mah back yard with guns drawn?"

Johnny Q switched to a more conciliatory tone. "I'm shuah sorry, man, I meant only respec'. This swindlin' low life owes me money." He pointed his gun at Senior, who was seeking to be one with the floor. "If you let me have him, we'll be out of here quicker than spit." He took a step towards his target.

"Not so fast, not so fast." Six hammers cocked on six guns. Johnny Q froze in his tracks. Buck turned to Senior, "Whatchya gotta say for yersel'?"

Thomas attempted to regain Buck's confidence, tough to accomplish while cowering under a table. "Not true, I won fair and square at poker. Ask anyone! Well, ask anyone else. You can't trust his cronies. Try Stanley Chase, he'll tell you honest."

The mention of Chase captured Hall's full attention. "Why? What's he got to do with the price of cotton?"

Senior climbed to his feet, glared at Johnny Q, then looked to his questioner. "Chase was playing too. Left as a winner, same as me. Johnny Q here is sore because he lost." He rounded on Johnny Q. "What was it, Johnny, a straight flush over four kings? You should be ashamed of yourself!"

Last night's loser stepped another pace forward, but the pistols dissuaded him. "I'll get you, mister, make no mistake, I'll get you!" He turned on his heel and strode out, attempting to gather his tattered dignity and authority.

Chapter 24

Thomas Senior breathed easily for the first time in hours. "Michael, it looks as though we've repelled Johnny Q, at least for the moment. Let's take a break and plan our next steps. Come on, I'll buy you a whiskey."

He gazed around the tent and found it lacking the comforts of a civilized inn. Instead of a fancy bar, three rough-hewn oak planks held half a dozen brown bottles surrounded by grimy glasses. And instead of a white-coated barman, there was Sweaty Betty, a hundred pounds overweight with big red hair and sore feet, shuffling between the tables. She had constructed her dress from a flour sack... or two... or three. There was the requisite footrest for a man to prop a boot. It was made of iron, not brass, but it served the purpose of easing the serious drinker's back fatigue. The saloon provided the spittoons so necessary here in the tobacco-raising south, although looking at the mahogany-stained floorboards nearby, southern gentlemen's aim left much to be desired.

The stewards from the *Ozark Queen* arrived and discarded the Thomas baggage in a corner.

Senior inspected the Raiders. Buck and three of his men had a few miles on Senior, inching into their sixties, beer-bellies preceding them. Their clothes were an incongruous mix of homespun and castoffs, with the odd piece of military uniform showing up in unusual places. Thomas noticed a gray kepi with the original bloodstains, while another Raider had a Union Army issue holster strapped to his waist. Buck had the prize, a Confederate officer's slouch hat with a yellow cord signifying that the hat at least had been closely involved with the Rebel cavalry.

The other two were much younger, near Junior's age. Their blond hair, prominent noses and lack of chins matched an elder Raider, making it obvious they were his sons. The lone drunk was better clothed and wasn't a professional tippler. Perhaps it was his way of dealing with a terrible day.

Senior donned his salesman persona. "Thanks for seeing them off, sir. Sore loser, eh? I'm glad he's gone; I'll tell you that for nothing. Thirsty work, though. Madam, bring me a glass of your best whiskey. Mr. Hall, will you join me? Gentlemen?" The Raiders checked with their leader, who nodded, and they bellied up to the bar. The proprietor hurried to serve her customers. Senior wiped the rim of his tumbler and took a cautious sip. "This is superb! Bourbon, is it? Must be, we're close enough to Kentucky, I fancy. Excellent taste, mellow too."

Buck interrupted. "I'm not interested in your opinion of our booze. Why are you here and how come you're lookin' for me?'

"Right. Randolph Washington said you'd help me. My son and I have business here in Rush, but need to go back to Batesville first. We can take care of ourselves, but it'd be prudent to enjoy the company of gentlemen such as you and your men who have local knowledge. There are rough individuals nearby." Thomas' pompous speech came naturally to him.

"Local knowledge, eh? Local guns too, I reckon. What's your business?"

"I own the Evening Star mine and I need to decide whether I should work it or sell it."

The drunk outsider at the bar raised his head and peered at Senior. He tried to point his finger and speak, but fell off his stool instead and scrabbled on the floor, struggling in vain to find his footing. The younger Raiders picked him up and pitched him into the street.

Buck continued his questioning. "How long are you figurin' on being in Batesville?"

"We'll ship out tomorrow, conduct my dealings the following morning, and return here later to conclude my affairs." Thomas added up the days. "I'll need your protection for a week."

"All of us?"

"Yes, all of you."

The Raiders grinned amongst themselves. The prospect of a steady income was stimulating.

"Five dollars a day. In advance."

"Deal!" Senior stuck out his hand. Buck looked at it, squinted at Thomas, decided money is money, no matter the source. He grabbed Thomas's fist and shook it with such vigor that the swindler thought his arm would come away from its socket. The con-man pulled out his wallet and counted off thirty-five dollars, which Buck tucked into his boot.

"You need me to keep your gamblin' friends from you?"

"That's right, and there's two other people I want you to watch for." Thomas described David and Tam as best he remembered from the brief encounter in the St. Louis station. "I expect they'll be arriving tomorrow from Batesville. There'll be a boat then, don't you think?"

"Weather permitting, yes. The water's goin' down fast. Why are they after you?"

"What's it to you?" Thomas didn't relish explaining himself to this rube.

"Nothin'. Curious is all. Anyone else after yer hide? It's getting to be quite the list."

"No, that's it. Your beaker is empty, Mr. Hall. Madam, fill 'em up, and one for yourself!" Thomas became expansive again now that he had protection surrounding him. It would have turned into a raucous party had Michael not whispered in Senior's ear. "Dad, we should settle into our hotel. We can drink with these folks this evening."

The eldest Raider boy, Caleb, slipped out the rear exit to check on the gambler and his gang. He returned within minutes. "Two of Johnny Q's band are watchin' the entrance to the pool hall, one at each end of the block, but there's nobody in the alley."

Buck made the decision on the Thomases' behalf. "Boss, here's what we're fixin' on doin'. Caleb here'll go out front and watch them. Buggs'll eyeball the alley. They'll let us know when it's safe. The pair of you'll be able to sneak out the back and check in."

At last, a plan worked as intended and soon the Thomases were relaxing in Senior's hotel room. The sons, Buggs and Caleb, stood guard outside the door. Senior, as usual, napped, leaving Junior to debate his decision. *Get out now while it's possible or wait for Da to pull off the mine ownership scam.*

Chapter 25

When the slant of the setting sun coursed around the bedroom and caught Senior square in the eyes, he stirred. "Son, what time is it? I'm hungry."

"It's after six, Pa. Let me ask the boys where to eat." Michael opened the door to question the brothers, returning moments later.

"They say there's a dining room here and, according to them," he jerked a thumb in the Raider boy's direction, "the food's good. Don't get your hopes up, though."

But this time it was Junior who was wrong. The hotel served excellent local fare ranging from steak to game to fish. Senior's trout was so succulent he asked for more. His son enjoyed a rich venison stew. A blackberry cobbler topped with freshly-churned ice cream finished the repast. Thomas paid for the Raiders' supper, albeit at a separate table. Based on their bony ribs and the speed with which their food disappeared, they hadn't eaten for days.

"I'm liking America more and more." Senior was relishing the warm pleasure of an outstanding meal. "Let's go back to the pool hall and sample more of that fine bourbon. And don't tell me no, boy! I plan on enjoying my evening with our new friends!"

The group stepped out into the dusk...and all hell broke loose.

A gunshot further up the narrow road chased a small herd of beef towards them. The loco cattle squeezed onto the wooden sidewalk, destroying everything in their path. Townsfolk scattered like startled minnows, climbing poles and dodging into backyards.

The stampede forced Junior, clutching the satchel as always, into an alley, separated for the moment from his Da and Buck's boys. A quick slash with a much-honed knife carved through the bag's strap. He didn't feel the second cut, which sliced his throat from ear-to-ear. He slumped to the ground, hidden by boxes from the dry goods store.

"Michael, Michael! Where are you?" Thomas had evaded the pandemonium by rolling under the walkway. "Buck, where's my son? Have your men find him!"

Caleb found Junior in the passageway by stumbling over him. "Bring a lamp, bring a lamp!"

Senior took one glance at Michael, his head almost severed, and vomited. Then, "Have you recovered the satchel?" Buck's followers searched the alleyway, with no success. "This is Johnny Q's work. Grab him! Five dollars to the man who brings him to me!" It wasn't revenge Thomas wanted; it was the money. The Raiders spread out while Senior and the leader of the Raiders stared at Junior's blood seeping through the alley's garbage.

Caleb again tracked the quarry. "Buck, Johnny Q and his gang stole a boat and set off downstream. Henry spotted them at the wharf and they had the bag."

"Whose boat do they have?"

"Flannigan's skiff. They took old Flannigan with them. He'll navigate the rapids a'right, but it'd be mighty dangerous at this hour of the night."

Buck turned to the hardly-grieving father. "We've lost him, I won't run the river in the dark." He emphasized his refusal with a shake of his head. "I suggest we take your boy to the undertaker. Once you've talked to him, we'll escort you to your room.

You can figure out what you're gonna do next in the morning." To Thomas' surprise, he added, "I'm sorry for your loss."

Chapter 26

The trip to the coffin maker with Michael's body sealed Senior's feelings. He made the necessary funeral arrangements, minimal though they were. After all, what church service speeds an avowed atheist on his way? Junior had listened well when Senior preached against religion, "There's no God, Michael. And no fate. We must make our own way in the world, with no help from Him."

Thomas retraced his steps to the hotel and paced the floor of his room. In seconds, his life had changed from prosperity and family to poverty and loneliness. For a moment, he teetered on the brink of anguish, but pulled himself back. *All right. Before I get too depressed, let's take stock. I have...,* he took out his ostrich-skin wallet and counted its contents, *a hundred dollars. That'll keep me going for a while.* True enough in a part of America where that was a good income for a year.

What else do I have? Damn, not much. Clothes, a decent watch, a snuffbox, nothing of actual value.

Thomas sat for a while, despair nibbling at the edges of his soul. *I wonder if Michael had cash or valuables in his luggage. His pockets were empty.* He surprised himself by choking up at the memory of his boy and the manner of his death. He shook his head. *I'll have time for grieving later. Now, where's his suitcase?*

Senior crossed the hallway to his son's room, nodding to the two Raiders still standing guard. He retrieved Michael's bag from the rough oak wardrobe, laid it on the bed and opened it. Picking up his boy's clothing piece by piece, he ran his fingers along the seams, hoping to detect concealed valuables. No luck. Again, the anguish clawed at his resolve. Again, he shoved it aside.

He picked up the top of the case to close it when he felt something slide, shifting the lid's weight. *Curious, what's that?* He reopened the valise, examined the lining of the lid and heard rustling. He found a slit in the seam in an inconspicuous place camouflaged by the checkered pattern. Thomas ripped the fabric apart, and there was a large brown envelope. *What the hell's this? Holy macaroni, it's my money...* He explored farther... *and the bonds! Hallelujah! I'm rich! I'm rich again!* And the *nouveau riche* father danced his jig, waving his finger, his feet capering over the worn-out carpet. He raised his eyes to the heavens. *Thank you, Michael, thank you,*

you devious son-of-a-gun, oh, bless you. You're a proper chip off the old block, aren't you? And every bit the equal of your brother. May you both rest in peace.

The enormity of his losses, the death of his sons, sank in at last and he collapsed into an easy chair, surrounded by his wealth, but all alone.

*   *   *

Johnny Q didn't find out he had a satchel full of newspapers (the ones Junior had gathered from the saloon on the *Ozark Queen* the night before), until first light, by which point he was hours downstream. His wrath was stunning.

"What the hell is this! Where's mah money? And what of the bearer bonds he's 'sposed to have?" Johnny Q smacked Duke in the face for not agreeing with him sufficiently and kicked another of his cronies overboard. "That stupid geezer isn't getting' the best of me. I'll kill him, that's what I'll do. I'll kill him!"

Duke chose not to point out that the river was in flood. It could be days before they'd be able to return to Rush in the skiff. Thomas might be anywhere.

Chapter 27

Brother George returned from his early morning walk to the San Francisco post office, brandishing a single envelope. "Mail for Miss Gordon! Mail for Miss Gordon!" he shouted as he entered his uncle's wee home.

Bella ran to him and snatched at the letter, but George held it above her reach while repeating his faux-postman call. "Mail for Miss Gordon!"

"George!" Bella pleaded, but her brother enjoyed the game... until she kicked him hard in the shin.

"Ouch! That hurt!"

Bella grabbed the longed-for message.

"Can't you take a joke?" George rubbed his leg while contemplating his revenge. Their mother shook her head. *Will they never grow up?*

The young lassie flew to the tool shed at the bottom of the small garden and plopped down on a weeding chair. She ripped the envelope open, but hesitated, afraid to read it. *What if he doesn't love me anymore? What if he's writing goodbye? Oh, I couldn't bear it!*

Smarten up, woman. Read the damned thing! Her alter ego chimed in with its usual sage advice.

Bella unfolded the three pages and absorbed David's message of devotion. She studied it a second time, more slowly, then a third, absorbing the details of his travels and of his feelings for her. She allowed her mind to roam back to the passionate kisses in the cabriolet circling Central Park, and forward to... what? *I still don't know if I can handle the duties of the wife of a noble.* She was debating that question when her parent sat down with her.

"Sweetie, from the roses in your cheeks, I'd say your letter held good news! Am I right?"

"Oh yes, Ma, it did." She described much of the contents of David's missive. "He didn't tell me when he'll arrive in San Francisco, and I can't wait!"

"That's grand that your letter arrived and was so positive." Fiona still had her misgivings regarding nobility's motives but had decided to provide support, at least outwardly. "And I hope your good fortune holds into this afternoon when you have your interview for the tutoring job."

"I haven't forgotten, Ma. It's with Mrs. Steben, isn't it? Tell me again what you learned of her. She's married to a railroad bigwig, has two children called William and Katie, and lives in an enormous villa in the hills. Is there anything else?"

"You forgot to say she was born in France."

"Yes, I'll bear that in mind." Bella's thoughts turned backwards. "What happened to the previous tutor?"

"The wee ones hated her. She was an old-school European and far too strict for today's world. Madame Steben found her using a rod on her young son. Can you imagine?"

"That's terrible! I would never do that."

Fiona pulled her back towards the house. "Come on, lass, you need to dress for your meeting." Bella tucked the love letter into her pocket and followed her Ma.

*   *   *

Mother and daughter stood outside the Steben villa in the weak afternoon sun. "What a handsome residence! Three stories, there has to be a dozen rooms or more. What do you think, Ma?"

"Aye, that's right, Bella, the house is bonnie, for sure. The grounds are impressive too; they remind me of Balmoral Castle back home. The Stebens must have a sizable staff to keep them so trim. I dunno architecture, but those pillars at the front door are imposing and elegant. These people can afford the best...you, for example, my dear."

Bella laughed with her parent. "I don't know about that, but thank you." She shifted to face the villa. "Time for me to meet Mrs. Steben. How do I look?" She pirouetted so Fiona could inspect her.

"Very smart, Bella! Very professional." Her mother examined her daughter's governess outfit, the polished black boots with a low heel, a black dress covering her ankles. The matching jacket fit snug over her crisp white blouse. Bella softened the severity of her appearance by adding a Gordon tartan choker. Her prize possession, the opal pendant Sir David had given her, flashed between her breasts.

"Thanks, Ma, I just wish I didn't have to wear this stupid hat!" She was referring to her large crimson bonnet, which was struggling to free itself and set sail on the afternoon breeze.

"Hold on to it until you get to the door. You'll take it off once you're indoors. Don't forget to use the servant's entrance. I expect it'll be in the rear."

Her daughter had a moment of panic. "Ma, please come with me!"

"No, dearie, we talked of this. You need to show the family you are a grown-up nineteen-year-old. Me going with you will make you appear to be a wee bairn, a nine-year-old. Now, chin up, shoulders back, and off you go. I'll wait here at the gate for you. Good luck!"

Chapter 28

Madame Patrice Steben watched the interchange between the Scottish women from her library window. Part of her interviewing practice was observing the applicants with their guard lowered. Yesterday, she'd rejected a candidate because the woman had been tippling from a flask before entering the Steben estate. *I'm not sure what I think of a potential tutor bringing a parent to an interview. On the other hand, it'll give me a chance to gauge how her own family interacts. And she's so young.*

Madame Steben opened the front door and called to Bella. "Miss Gordon, please, come in this way."

Bella mounted the three steps to the main entrance, held her head high and smiled. She clasped Madame Steben's extended hand and bobbed a curtsy.

"Miss Gordon, I am Patrice Steben, how do you do?"

"Very well, thank you, Ma'am. And you?"

"I too am fine. May I ask, did someone accompany you today, your mother perhaps?"

"You're correct, Madame. It is my mother, Fiona."

"I can't have her standing in the street while we speak. Elizabeth!" She called over her shoulder, and a maid appeared. "Please go to the front gate and find out if Mrs. Gordon..." Patrice cocked an eye at Bella for confirmation, who nodded. "will join you for tea in the lounge while Miss Gordon and I chat. We'll meet with her later. Now, dear, Miss Gordon, come this way."

Patrice led Bella to the back of the house where a large conservatory overlooked the surrounding hillsides. The young Scot gasped. The room was bright and airy of course, but it was crammed with a vibrant mixture of tropical flowers, including hibiscus, birds of paradise and orchids. The scent from the blooms was intoxicating.

"What a lovely room, Ma'am! I've never seen such beauty!" A branch covered with crimson blossoms caught her attention. "What's the name of this plant?"

"It's a bougainvillea from Brazil. You have excellent taste. Other than the orchids, it's my favorite."

"Which are they?"

The lady of the house pointed to the specific section of the hothouse. "*Voila!* There!"

"*Mervellieux!* Marvelous!"

Mrs. Steben looked at her. "I didn't know you spoke French."

"Yes, Madame, my college required we speak nothing but French one day of the week. We called it *Francais Friday.*"

Patrice launched into a conversation in her native language about Bella's education, her favorite topics and subjects, her experience. Bella responded in the same language, answering fully without hiding any details, including her minimal history as a governess.

"Why don't we have a cup of tea. Elizabeth! Bring tea for two...and the chocolate eclairs." The maid scooted off to the kitchen.

Patrice smiled at her visitor. "There goes my waistline, but I sense it's for a good cause."

"Ma'am, at the risk of sounding like a sycophant, you don't look as though you need to worry." She was correct. Patrice was tall, elegant, and slim, the epitome of a San Francisco socialite. Her pompadour hairstyle, enhanced by a twist knot, highlighted her auburn hair. Her clothes, sophisticated and tasteful, enhanced her beauty.

"Flattery will get you anywhere, *ma cherie!* Ah, here's the tea and eclairs. Will you pour please?"

While Bella did the honors, Patrice examined the young lass. *She's a breath of fresh air: pleasant, intelligent, well-educated. I feel a connection with her that's been sadly lacking with the other candidates. She seems trustworthy, but I have to watch her interact with my babies before I overlook her lack of experience.* "Bella, do you wish to visit with my children?"

Bella's eyes lit up. "Please, Madame. I'd love to. Their names are William and Katie, I believe?"

"You've done your homework." Patrice called for them. "Here they are."

Two rambunctious children burst into the greenhouse and fidgeted by their mother's side.

"William, Katie, say hello to Miss Gordon. She wishes to talk with you."

"And you can talk to me. Ask me anything." Bella knelt so she could face them eye-to-eye.

William started. "Do you use the rod or the strap?"

His mother blanched and moved to interrupt, but Bella halted her with a slight shake of her head. "Neither, William. I don't hold with punishing my pupils. There's something wrong with my teaching if my pupil requires scolding. The fault would be mine. So, no, I never hit anyone."

"You're so young, what can you teach us?" Katie's turn.

"That's right, I am young. But I was taught in one of the best learning systems in the world. Do you know where Scotland is?"

Two heads shook in unison.

"If I become your tutor, I'll show you on a globe. It's in Europe and we'll go all over Europe in our imagination. We'll eat the foods and sing the songs and learn the languages, especially French, your *Maman's* home tongue."

Katie left her mother's side, tip-toed to Bella, and crept into her lap. "Please stay and be our tutor, Miss Gordon."

Bella's tears matched Patrice's.

"Your *Maman* and I have more to discuss but I really, really want to be your teacher!"

"Good." said William, "It's settled!"

Chapter 29

"Where are we, Tam? Is every mining camp this chaotic?" Sir David and his mentor had disembarked from the *Jessie Blair* and stood at the foot of the ramp, inspecting Rush's tent city haphazardly sprawling on the river shelf and clambering up the sides of the valley. The tents were of countless sizes and shapes. Some were mere tarpaulins strung between trees while others were attached to Conestoga wagons. Tam spied a few civil war relics with matching bullet holes. Hundreds of shelters competed for a spot.

The energy and movement of the scene suggested an upturned anthill to David. Men washed up after a shift in the mines, women cooked over open fires, children played, dogs scavenged. The camp was noisy, too, laughter, singing, shouting, fighting. But the barrenness of the land made the greatest impact. The nearest forests were miles away. After the lush greenery they had enjoyed on board the sternwheeler, the stark landscape assaulted their senses.

"I don't know if all camps are the same, but I imagine many are. I suppose they clear the woods to allow space for the workers' shacks."

"Or to feed the steam engines. Look." David pointed to a giant plume of smoke hanging over the canyon in the stillness of the early evening. "It doesn't sound as though they're working."

"It's Saturday and after six. I'm sure the miners have quit for the day. I'd guess the pool room will be full. There, beside the store."

They grabbed their bags, walked over to Sweaty Betty's and pushed past the canvas flap. Tam was right. Patrons crowded the saloon to capacity and beyond, but as the two friends crossed the threshold, the drinkers fell silent as if expecting the newcomers' arrival. Like the parting of the Red Sea, the crowd inched to the side, leaving a pathway to the bar. At the end of the channel, the Raider sons, Caleb and Buggs, turned last night's drunk upside down and held him by the ankles.

"Hey, Sir David! Here's your minin' engineer! Make a wish!" They pulled the drunk's legs apart until he howled in agony.

The Scots stared at each other, puzzled. *So much for traveling incognito.* thought David. *And who's this engineer?*

He stepped towards the Raiders, but his friend restrained him. "I've got this."

Tam strolled forward; the boys dropped the engineer-in-question and prepared for battle. *Two against one, how tough could it be?*

As he closed on the callow men, Tam, smiling, said, "Gentlemen," and stuck out his hand to shake Caleb's. The youngster, out of age-old courtesy, took it... and Tam upended his life.

He gripped Caleb's hand and shoved it lower. The Raider resisted by pulling it up, Tam reversed his thrust and drove it even higher until it was chest height. He ducked under his foe's elbow, slipped behind him, rammed the arm up between his shoulder blades and swept his feet out from under him. Caleb landed nose-first on the floor. Tam tugged his limb further up his torso until the ligaments gave. Caleb screamed.

His brother came awake and scrambled for his gun. Tam drove his leg out, kicking Buggs hard on the knee. The joint collapsed and his opponent crumbled, shrieking in pain.

Tam stood up... and Buck Hall shot him in the back.

Chapter 30

The force of the shot threw Tam's body onto a poker table, sending the chips flying. The six players scrambled to pick up the tokens, joined by onlookers who no doubt palmed as many as possible. Other patrons rushed to get out of the line of fire, while a ghoulish few pressed forward to stare at Tam... or his corpse. At least one barrel-shaped customer bolted out the rear door, leaving ill-will in his wake. The chaos meant David couldn't reach his friend. Tiring of being polite, he powered a path through the crowd, shouting "Debris! Debris!" as he went. Buck Hall heard him and put up his gun, telling his three healthy comrades to follow his lead.

Tam yelled. "Beggar it!" Followed by "Shoot a man in the back, would you, you cretin! I'll carve you into pieces and feed you to the hogs! I'll tie you to the nearest tree and smear you with honey and have the ants eat you alive! I'll..."

David sighed with relief. By this point, he had barged his way to his friend's side. "Tam, where are you hit? Are you hurting?"

The old warrior's right hand pressed his chest. Blood seeped through his fingers. Shock was settling in and Tam's rage had passed, in part because he was having a hard time breathing. "The bullet's gone through and through. That's good news." He stopped to draw a breath. "But I need you to tell me what you see. Is there anything pink and frothy showing?" He relaxed his pressure for a moment.

"No, it's deep red, a steady stream, and not as much as I expected. Why?"

Tam drew a shallow mouthful of air. "If the blood's foamy, it means a damaged lung. That would be awfy bad." He grimaced. "If the bullet didn't leave any of my clothing in there, I'll be fine. No thanks to this imbecile!" His voice rose once again as he spotted the senior Raider peering over David's shoulder.

"Why the hell are you crying 'Debris'?" Buck retorted, pistol still cocked and pointed towards David.

"Randolph Washington messed up and gave your name to a villain called Thomas, who later tried to cheat him. He told us the code to stop you from believing the crook or providing him with protection. I'll explain everything once I have Tam's injury checked. Is there a doctor in Rush?"

A card player got off his knees, wiped his pants, gave up on his futile search for the rest of his chips. "Yes, I'm the doctor. Matheson, at your service." He was of medium height, slim, had a mop of white hair with a black cowlick in front and the ruddy complexion of an outdoorsman. "What your friend said is true. The biggest concern with a through and through wound, assuming no damage to organs or bones, is putrefaction from any fabric left hidden. Let me examine him. Here, help me." Four able-bodied miners lifted his new patient on top of the bar.

David was torn between wanting to be with Tam and the physician, and needing to talk to Buck Hall. He was keen to find out Thomas Senior's whereabouts, and here was "his" mining engineer, the wishbone from earlier, trying to grab his coat sleeve.

"Breathe, David, breathe," he told himself.

Chapter 31

*A*ll right. The young noble took stock. *The doctor appears sober and competent, so Tam's in safe hands. There's nothing useful for me to do there. Next, I want Buck to tell me of his discussions with Thomas. But first, I'll talk to the engineer.* "What's your name, sir? And how are your legs?"

"Williams, Sir David, John Williams. They're fine, no thanks to Mr. Hall here." He glowered at the old Raider, who scowled back.

The Scot heard the Welsh lilt match the Welsh surname. "I've to meet with Buck, then the doctor. Afterwards, I promise, you and I will visit. Does that suit you?"

"Yes, Sir David." The engineer's eyes gleamed. "I assure you what I have to report is to your significant advantage."

David gave him a thoughtful appraisal, then turned to talk to the leader of the Raiders. He told Buck of meeting Randolph and Randolph's description of Thomas Senior trying to cheat him. David also recounted how the buckboard driver regretted giving Buck's name and therefore protection, to Thomas.

Buck growled, "Randolph's a decent fella even if he has gone straight. He deserved better than that." He pulled on his chin whiskers. "Maybe that crook didn't pay me enough to protect him." Buck's moral agility showed up loud and clear. "Where is he?" He peered round the pool hall.

"Thomas is here?" David's anger ratcheted up a notch.

"He was when your lot appeared. Boys, find him and bring him to me."

David checked with Doc. Matheson while Buck's men hunted Thomas. "How's he doing, Doctor?"

"Well, I can't be certain, but I think his own diagnosis is correct. It's a clean wound with no damage to internal organs. Your man's correct to be concerned about clothing. I haven't found remnants, but the bullet may have left shredded cloth in its path." Doc. Matheson squinted into Tam's chest. "I need stronger light than this. Can we move him to my surgery?"

"Of course. You'll want help. Gentlemen!" David nodded to the four who had lifted his partner onto the bar. "Thanks for your aid earlier. If you carry my associate to Doc Matheson's, there'll be a dollar in it for you."

The miners rushed to provide the necessary transport while David bent over Tam. "Take care, my friend. You're in expert hands. I'll be along to check on you." Tam's face was white with shock. He managed a brief nod.

Buck was ready with Thomas's whereabouts. "He isn't here. When your man started fightin' my lads, he ran out the rear door, grabbed a wagon and took off out-of-town looking for the railhead." Buck grinned, a frightful thing to see, what with half his teeth missing and the rest rotten and tobacco-stained. "The problem is, he went south, the wrong way. The trail he chose is a stump road. He's stranded in the forest tonight with snakes and bears and bugs to keep him company. He'll be easy pickin's in the morning."

"Are you sure I can catch him tomorrow? He has property of mine I must recover."

"You mean his satchel? He lost that to a card shark."

"He gambled it away? I don't believe it!"

"Nah, the gamblers stole it."

Chapter 32

Buck explained to David how Johnny Q had stolen the satchel and its contents. (The Raider didn't know that Junior had replaced the cash and bonds with newspapers before he died.)

David was crushed. He pushed past the shooter and paced the floor; the miners giving him a wide berth. His trip to Arkansas had started with the two objectives of saving his father's estate by securing the proprietorship of the mine, and recovering as much as possible from Thomas. Now, with the loss of the valise, pursuing the ownership appeared to be his only choice. On a positive note, he'd seen with his own eyes that Rush was a booming town, increasing the likelihood that his land had value. Which reminded him of "his" Welsh engineer.

"Excuse me, Buck, I need to talk to Mr. Williams." David paused. "By the way, I'll be hunting Thomas at first light and I lack a guide. Do you know someone who'd be interested? I'd pay."

Buck rubbed his hands. "Let me come, Sir David, five dollars a day." His parents had named 'Buck' well. "Be here at six. You can have my other horse." The old brigand turned away to tend to his injured Raiders.

David beckoned to his mining engineer. "Now, Mr. Williams, your turn. Who are you and what information do you have for me regarding my mine?"

"Let's sit outside... fewer ears, you understand." The Welshman led him to a comfortable bench under an ancient oak. Darkness was falling, and the tent city was quietening for the night. "First, I'm a miner from north Wales."

"I recognize the accent, Mr. Williams, but I didn't know Wales mined silver?"

"It doesn't, Sir David. There's no silver here either, but both mines have one thing in common... zinc, tons of the mineral."

"What! The mine my father bought produced silver, not zinc." The young man's voice rose. "You told me you had good news. Now would be a good time to share with me." He scowled at the engineer.

"Wait, Sir! Wait! I do have positive news. But allow me tell you the mine's history. Five or six years ago, three men, who weren't miners, purchased the Evening Star. They extracted a limited amount of ore and had it assayed. The report suggested eight per cent silver, which made it a very rich find." Williams grinned to himself. "Or so they thought."

David asked. "What do you mean?"

"The proprietors built a small smelter, loaded it with the raw mineral and fired it up, expecting the precious metal to run into the catch basins. But that's not what happened. All that showed was a rainbow of colors as the zinc flared. The tapped-out owners became discouraged and tried to peddle the Evening Star, still as a silver mine, but had no takers. I believe the final asking price was one box of smoked oysters!"

"I'm still waiting for a 'significant advantage', sir." David kept telling himself, *Don't shoot the messenger!* but the disappointments, shocks and fear were building.

"Right. Around this time, Baron Tookov bought your Star for pennies, sight unseen. He in turn sold it to your father as a silver mine, using the erroneous survey as bait. Tookov didn't realize he was sitting on an extremely rich mother lode, except it was zinc, not silver."

David's anxiety diminished. "You're well-informed of the mines and their owners. How so?"

"You're correct, sir, I am. Are you aware that your father's mine borders the Morning Star, the most successful operation hereabouts?"

"Yes, Broderick in Batesville told me."

"Until yesterday, I was its engineer, Stanley Chase's right-hand man. We've been keeping tabs on who owns your property because we, I mean 'he, Chase', wants to buy it."

"Why 'until yesterday'?"

"Because he sacked me." The miner mumbled a sudden outburst of Welsh, curse words, no doubt.

"And why did he sack you?"

"He ordered me to tunnel into your property from our side of the boundary. We were working a rich vein that continues into your land and he wanted me to extract it, despite it not being ours. I refused, saying it was theft, Chase got mad and gave me the boot. I came to Sweaty Betty's last evening to drown my sorrows when who should appear, but this Tookov or Thomas character, claiming to be the owner. I pegged him for a fraud at once, but I was kicked out before I could confront him. Then I heard you were in pursuit and put two and two together."

"So…" David let the next words hang while he collected his thoughts. "what do you estimate my mine to be worth?" The critical question, he waited for the critical answer.

"As I said, I can be of great help to you." Williams smiled.

The young Scot had to laugh. Here he was being shaken down again. "You need to give me at least an idea of the mine's value before I figure out how to compensate you."

"That's true." the Welshman admitted. He paused to gather his thoughts. "Allow me to explain it this way. In the mining world, one method of valuing a company is to examine its revenues for the past years. The Evening Star has none…" Williams' turn to let a sentence hang. "But the Morning Star does. Last year, its earnings were over a million dollars. Because your property is adjacent, and because the richest vein runs through it, your mine is worth at least the same, a million dollars!"

David collapsed into a chair, swallowing hard, his thoughts racing in every direction. *Assuming I sell the property, I can repay my father with interest and my obligation to him will be complete. And to his solicitor and accountant. I want to go after Thomas. I could say it's justice I'm seeking, but revenge is my true motive. I'll take care of Tam, then find Bella. There's another idea tickling the back of my mind. I can't give form to it yet, I want to think on it more. Or, rather, not think of it, allow it to surface on its own accord.*

"Mr. Williams, how earnest is Chase's interest in my mine?"

"Desperate, Sir David, desperate. His fellow-investors are pushing him hard because they expect the demand for zinc to escalate. You're aware of the saber-rattling going on in Europe nowadays?"

"Ah, the winds of war, yes, I understand. Let me mull over what you've said. You did, eventually," David grinned, "bring me excellent advice. You'll get a handsome reward. But I have other ideas I need to explore. I'm chasing Thomas in the morning and expect to return in one or two days. Will you meet me here tomorrow night or, if I don't show, the next night?"

"Of course. I'll be happy to. And I'll be sober."

Chapter 33

"Mr. Williams, can you point me towards Doctor Matheson's office?"

"Let me take you there, it's nearby. This way."

David and the engineer strode to the surgery in the gathering of the night, the young noble asking questions involving mining and the journey the Welsh couple had taken to end up in Rush.

"This is a beautiful part of the world, Sir David. My wife and I enjoy living here. Or we did, until Chase became greedy. Here you are, here's Doc's house. Where are you staying?"

"I haven't got that far yet. What do you suggest?"

"The company hotel is the best in town, but my ex-boss owns it and hears all that happens, so if you're seeking privacy," he glanced at David's clothes, "I'd look elsewhere."

"I'm past caring about going incognito, if that's what you mean. I'll accept your recommendation."

"Tell them I sent you, they'll take care of you. Good night, Sir David. I trust you'll find your man in acceptable form."

Tam was better than David had feared. Dr. Matheson had examined the wound and declared it to be clean. He'd applied a salve, a recipe from a local Indian tribe, and was bandaging Tam's upper torso when David arrived. Marthe Fontana, a handsome widow woman, assisted the doctor and would nurse the old soldier back to health if it were the last thing she did. David smiled, his companion had landed on his feet again. A pang of loneliness followed as he allowed himself to think of Bella for a moment.

"Doctor, what's the verdict? Will he live?"

"Yes, I expect so. Your man is in excellent physical shape and the bullet missed anything vital so he'll make a complete recovery."

Tam growled. "Hey, I'm right here. I can hear everything. When do I get out of here?" He tried to sit up, but Marthe put her hand on his chest to keep him flat.

"All in good time, Mr. McKenzie, all in good time. You should be fit to leave in two weeks."

"Two weeks? What am I to do here for two weeks?" He relaxed into his pillow, muttering that he'd be out of there in two days at the latest.

David seized the opportunity to inform Tam that he planned on hunting Thomas the next day. Tam protested that he must go with him, but even the complaining tired him and he surrendered to David's chasing the crook on his own.

Chapter 34

David and Buck set off at first light to track Thomas Senior. Though the skies were cloudless now, it had rained hard in the wee small hours of the morning and sucked away yesterday's zest and vitality. The tent city looked bedraggled and sullen, challenging the spirit of the hardiest family. Rivulets grew into streams, then into creeks. The Buffalo River was rising, carrying cut timber along with freshly-toppled trees. *I'm lucky I arrived yesterday; the Jessie Blair wouldn't make it today.* The landscape was changing before him.

He had stopped at the surgery and found that Tam had been restless through the night. Despite the early hour, Doc Matheson had already examined his friend's wound and prescribed more of the Indian liniment, allowing his patient to relax and fall into a deep sleep. All-in-all, the doctor was pleased with his patient.

Aye, David thought, *your patient but my friend.*

*　　*　　*

"Well, Buck, what's the plan?"

"We'll head for the woods over there." Buck nodded towards the distant tree line where forests still stood despite man's best efforts to denude the land. "There's a trailhead leading to the Varner Mine and we follow it until we find him. It climbs Gage Bluff over by the river. He won't have gone far in the cart; he wasn't a horseman. But the creeks worry me. We've had a heavy rain in the past few days and the water's risin'. That'll stop him for sure, but we might end up on the wrong side of a creek also. Watch where you put your mount. It's dangerous at the best of times, but today's conditions are worse, what with the mud."

David saw what Buck meant when he said their quarry couldn't have traveled far. The stump road was well named. The mine employees had cut the trees low to the ground, but left the stumps in place; a cart's axle would barely clear them. It'd be tough going for an experienced driver, let alone a neophyte like Thomas, and impossible in the dark. David's spirits rose. Senior was close and the conclusion to this chase was likely to come soon.

"I've brought this for you should Thomas try an ambush." The Raider drew a rifle from the saddle holster and gave it to the young Scot, along with a pouch of bullets. David scrutinized it, a Winchester 1873. He'd heard of "The Gun that Won the West," but this was his first time handling one. Buck showed him how it functioned and David test-sighted it, swinging the barrel towards imaginary targets.

"This feels comfortable. How true does it shoot?"

"A slight pull to the right, nothing to worry you except on long shots. It'll cost you forty dollars plus another fifty for Blaze, your colt."

David had to admire the ease with which the Raider changed from guide to pirate. "Buck, both horse and gun are old and used. You're asking top dollar for them and they're not worth it. Here's thirty."

Buck grinned. "You got someplace else to buy firearms, Mister? All right, I'll be reasonable, seein's how I likes you. Seventy-five."

"Forty." He responded, ignoring the implied threat.

"Done."

"Buck, here's twenty, you get the rest when I'm through with Thomas."

The horses picked their path over the roots and stumps. It was much too slow for David; he wanted to catch Senior and finish the business. But he knew the danger of pushing too hard. He'd have to stay calm and enjoy his surroundings.

Arkansas was putting on a brilliant display for him. The recent rains fresh-scrubbed the countryside, leaving it glistening in the morning light. The fall foliage was reaching its peak, and mist rose from the valleys as the sun worked its way around to warm them. The wildlife was active as usual at this hour. David listened to the crows singing in three-part disharmony, which transported him back to Ballboyne. He recalled hunting with Tam for Leviathan, the magnificent stag. So similar, yet poles apart. That day was a world distant and a century past and came from an innocent time. And the quarry was different.

The pursuers were high on a hill bordering the river when David drew on the reins. He had a clear view of the trail half a mile ahead as it avoided a crag by plunging into the valley. Then the road vanished behind the shoulder of a steep spur drooping from the hillside.

"Buck, is that movement?" He pointed to a spot near the riverbank.

Buck reined in his mare. "My eyes ain't as good as they used to be. I can't see nuthin'."

David sighed in exasperation. *Why did I bring him along if he can't see?* "There, east of the spine running south from the cliff."

"Sorry, Sir David, nuthin'."

David dismounted and fished his new spotting scope from inside his jacket. *My spotting scope. The glass that saved my life. Was that less than a month ago? Concentrate, David, concentrate.* He steadied the scope on the branch of a tree, focused, and breathed a sigh of relief. *Yes, it's Thomas right enough. He's making pitiful progress with the buckboard. We've got him!* He pulled the Winchester out of its holster, eager to deal with his nemesis before he disappeared. *A six-hundred-yard shot with an untested rifle? Difficult, but not impossible.* He was fumbling in his pocket for the box of cartridges when Buck grabbed the barrel of his gun and thrust it skywards.

"David, don't kill him in cold blood, no matter how much he deserves it. You'll carry the burden for the rest of your days." Buck's eyes darted to his left, counting his ghosts. "You won't need me anymore; we'll meet at Sweaty Betty's tonight. Here, this stuff's for the bugs." Buck dropped a can of goo into

David's surprised hands. Before David could voice his protest, Buck wheeled his horse and started back to Rush.

David watched him leave but decided Buck was correct, he wasn't needed. He also concluded that Buck's advice was sound. Killing a man, even Thomas, was profoundly different than hunting deer. Or defending oneself.

Chapter 35

Peter Thomas Senior stretched and groaned in agony, his flabby body ill-designed for sleeping in the back of a buckboard. Sleep?! Hah! He hadn't slept a wink. Night creatures had kept him awake and on edge...snuffling, slithering, squeaking, hooting, prowling and growling, none of which he saw through the persistent rain. And the bugs! He itched all over, his arms, legs, even his thighs where beasties had climbed up his pants and enjoyed a bite. His face was the worst. He felt as though he'd been on the wrong end of a 25-round heavyweight championship fight: raw, bloodied, painful and so swollen he was almost blind.

He was, however, making progress. Since dawn, he'd put more miles between himself and Rush. That was the good news. But now he faced the toughest obstacle yet, a fast-running creek with steeper banks than previously encountered.

The stream rumbled down the hillside, then flattened out for ten yards where it crossed the trail, before plunging to the Buffalo River a hundred feet below.

The sheer hill on his right was covered with thick clumps of bush and vines. The occasional tree, defying gravity, hung on for dear life with its roots gnarled around the rocks. On the other side of the torrent, the route was obvious, but the creek's sides were precipitous and unforgiving. Descending the bank, crossing the swift-flowing stream and climbing out would require a heroic feat. Thomas thought a swim was the probable result... a swim with a steep drop.

Choices? None, cross or be caught. I assume David-bloody-Rennie is following me. If I make it across, and the flood continues to rise, I might be safe from him. But I'll have to ditch the buckboard. I'll never reach the other bank with it in tow. Gorblimey, the water's rising fast! Time to go. Come on, Dobbin, let's get you unhitched.

But first, he draped the two precious saddlebags around his neck and secured them. Then Thomas released Dobbin from the cart, taking twice as long as anyone with a smidgen of knowledge of buckles and straps and tack. He did leave the reins on, but still dreaded the thought of riding his horse bareback. *Nothing for it, Peter me lad, onward!*

He clambered aboard and wound his hands through the bridle and the horse's mane, shouted "Tallyho!" at the top of his lungs and spurred his steed on with his heels. His mount entered the spirit of things and launched himself across the torrent. His front hooves fell short of dry land, but his momentum caused him to stagger forward and right himself.

Thomas tumbled sideways into the swollen creek which swept him to the brink of the waterfall. He lost his grip on his horse's mane but, more by good luck than good management, kept his hands entwined in the harness. Dobbin scrambled onto shore and arrested Thomas's progress towards the rim of the falls, but the crook came close to drowning in the process. He was spinning in the rushing water like a giant but exotic fish bait, with his head rarely above water. At last, he found his footing and pulled himself up the straps inch by inch to dry land.

Thomas lay there, coughing and retching and cursing any and all Rennies. but had enough wit to crawl behind a bush in case Sir David appeared.

He conducted a quick self-appraisal. *I've got the saddlebags. Wet, obviously. I'm glad I wrapped the money and bonds in oilskin. In pain, my knee isn't working and is bleeding. The dunking has lessened the itch of the insect bites, but they'll return. I have my wallet and watch. And I'm exhausted.* He sighed. *I need to rest for a moment before I go on.* Thomas passed out.

Chapter 36

David and Blaze continued their pursuit. They were on the same road as Thomas and within striking distance. Brilliant! But the heat from the sun raised the humidity to distressing levels, leaving both of them sweating like an old sock. He looked forward to cooling himself in the next creek. But his primary discomfort was insects of all shapes, sizes and colors. David had never seen such a variety, ranging from gnats, irritating for their affinity for his nostrils, to big green flying beetles. And mosquitoes. Millions and millions of the beggars, all hungry. He spread Buck's ointment on his exposed skin and found it worked despite, or because of, the appalling smell.

Another hour passed with no trace of his quarry, but David knew he was gaining; he felt it in his belly. The trail led him out of the valley and back to the side of a spur where he came to his biggest obstacle yet, an untamed torrent flowing fast and high. And there was Thomas's abandoned buckboard! David's excitement ratcheted up a notch as he scanned the trees for a trap. No sign of his nemesis.

Fresh horse tracks entered the creek, emerged on the far side and disappeared behind a copse of aspens. A perfect place for an ambush. *Mmmh, what are my options?* David heard Tam's training. *Give up? No way! Take a run at the torrent with Buck's horse? The water's risen. It must be ten inches deeper than when Thomas crossed, based on the spoor. And the banks are very steep. We'd wash over the cliff before we climbed out. Wait for the flood to dissipate? Buck called these flash floods, but it might be days before the streams disperse. Leave Blaze here and catch up with Thomas on foot? Possible. I travel faster than he can on horseback, and he can't be a mile ahead of me. But I still need to cross here. Mmmh.*

He examined the hillside on his right. The vines caught his eye. He picked up the end of one and yanked on it. It didn't break, just cut into his hands. An idea formed. He sawed through three long creepers, plaited them into a rope which he anchored to a sturdy oak. He left himself enough to span the stream and to tie around his waist.

I'll go upstream, jump as far as I can, and swim like hell. If I don't make it across, the vines'll keep me from washing into the Buffalo. I need to toss

*over my Winchester, it's got to stay dry. But first I'm
going to look after Blaze.*

David secured his horse to a branch and
unsaddled him. "You've done well, old chum, but
you're staying here." He stroked Blaze's nose. "You
have shade, water and grass. I'll be back shortly,
you'll be fine." Blaze found a patch of greenery to his
liking and munched away.

David heaved the Winchester over the stream,
making sure it landed flat on a patch of sod beside
the waterfall. The young Scot turned to the vine
cable, wrapped it around his torso and knotted a
bowline.

"Why thank you! Sir David, I presume?"

Chapter 37

Blaze's soft nickering roused Thomas Senior. He was exhausted from his rough night spent in the great outdoors, and from picking his way through the maze of stumps. This morning's dousing and beating in the creek had left him at the end of his willpower.

The horse whinnied again. Then he heard David's Scottish brogue soothing the colt. "Damn it to hell! It's Sir David!" He pulled himself upright, and peered through a blackberry bush. "Yes, it's him!" Fear had risen in his throat. "How can I best Rennie? My only weapon's the knife I found in the buckboard."

Then the young noble tossed his gun across the stream. Thomas pounced on it.

*   *   *

David whipped round towards the sound. There was Senior, standing on the patch of grass, cradling the recently airborne Winchester in both hands.

So this is Peter Thomas, alias Baron Tookov. David inspected the man in front of him. *I'm not impressed. His fancy clothes are wet, mud-splattered and torn. He's bleeding from a gash on his leg. And his hair's sticking out in every direction, making him look like a fat rag doll. Ah! There's a pair of muddy saddlebags slung over his shoulder. He's clutching them as though they're valuable. Could it be...?* He attempted to squash his excitement.

David squinted at Senior's face. It was as swollen as a bullfrog, thanks to the ravenous appetites of the mosquitoes. Despite Thomas's calm demeanor, the Scot recognized a man nearing collapse. A night alone in the woods will do that to a citified dandy.

David's emotions sharpened by several notches. "Why, Baron Tookov, what a surprise. I thought you'd have traveled farther."

"No, I'm planning on returning to Rush."

"Haven't you enjoyed your time in the wild?" David baited the swindler. Desperate and unhinged men do stupid things.

"Enjoy it? How the hell could I enjoy anything? The bugs drove me insane, my face feels like a football, and savage animals stalked me. Then there was the rain. I'm soaked through and through. I'll be glad to get back to civilization, I can tell you. A pity you'll never see it again." Thomas raised the Winchester.

The Scot took a step and launched himself over the creek, adrenalin fueling his leap, splash-landing four feet short of the far bank.

Thomas was so surprised he almost forgot to shoot...almost. David was so close that Thomas didn't need to aim, merely point and pull the trigger.

Chapter 38

Nothing happened!

Thomas pulled the trigger again. And again. Still nothing.

David fought through the current and scrambled up the slope, cutting the vines around his waist as he reached the bank. In desperation, Thomas threw the rifle at his pursuer and, more by good luck than good aim, caught David square on the forehead. Stunned, the Scot fell into the creek where the torrent carried him towards the cascades.

The con artist didn't wait to see David's fate, but limped along the trail until he was out of sight.

The sudden dousing cleared the younger man's head, yet the rapids swept him to the edge of the falls. Instead of fear, rage claimed him. "I'll be damned before I let Thomas best me! Damn him to hell!" He saw a branch sticking out over the water and grabbed it with his left hand. The torrent carried his body over the brink, and he dangled in space for what seemed like an eternity. The bough gave way a smidgeon, and his heart surged into his mouth. *Please, hold a little longer.* He spied and grasped a root, and at last his feet found purchase on the rocks. Inch by careful inch, he dragged himself onto dry land, keeping an eye open for Thomas.

He recovered the Winchester, picked a box of waterproof cartridges out of his jacket pocket and inserted them into the breech. *Did that citified dandy expect me to toss a loaded gun? What an idiot! Now, where is he?"*

On high alert, David followed the road, expecting an ambush at any moment. And he was correct. He had hardly rounded the first bend when he heard pebbles dislodge on the hillside to his right.

Thomas jumped from his hiding place behind a bush, the Bowie knife heading for David's throat. Tam's training kicked in: *do the unexpected.* Rather than backing up, he leapt forward and blocked his enemy's wild slash with his forearm. He dipped his body, and braced himself for the oncoming collision. Thomas, unhealthy and unprepared, hit the younger man's shoulder with his breastbone, bounced off and collapsed with the wind knocked out of him. While he gulped and retched, struggling to suck air into his lungs, David stepped on Senior's wrist, pried the blade out of his hand and tossed it over the precipice into the Buffalo River. Next, he seized the saddle bags, ignoring Thomas's weak protest.

"What's in here then?"

Thomas hadn't the breath to answer. He made halfhearted gestures with his hands, scrabbling to retrieve the panniers from David's grasp.

The Scot backed out of range and opened an oilskin-wrapped parcel from one of the bags. Cash! Lots and lots of cash! New and old, clean and dirty notes, ones and fives and tens and twenties and hundreds. A surge of relief swept through David as he realized his journey had been worthwhile. Here was enough money to rescue his father's estate and compensate the solicitor and accountant.

He opened the other bag and discovered the Bearer Bonds. Dozens and dozens of them. A quick glance showed values that overwhelmed him. He'd need to give the bonds much more thought.

Thomas's breathing had become less labored, and he was attempting to stand. The young Scot put a foot on his chest, pinning him to the ground.

David recalled the investors Thomas had bilked, and, once again, David's anger worked its way to the surface. "You're a miserable excuse for a human being, aren't you? I can't think of one good reason why I should let you live."

"Please Sir David, please! I..."

"Don't 'Please Sir David' me!" His shouting was effective too; coveys of birds were fleeing the confrontation. "What a parasite you are, preying on the weak and feeble! *You* swindled Lord Rennie, dragged me to this ill-begotten scrap of earth and caused Buck to shoot my friend!" He took his foot off Thomas's chest and stepped backward. "Get up! Get up, you wretched thief! Go wait over there! I'm not wasting my energy rolling you over the bluff when I finish with you. On your feet, you coward!" David screamed, emphasizing each point with a stab of his Winchester. He was quite enjoying the part he was playing. "Is there a record of the people you've swindled?"

"What...? I don't...?"

"Did you keep records of your victims?" Still shouting.

"Yes, I kept a ledger." Thomas was on his knees but reluctant to rise any further.

"Where? Where is it?" He poked the older man hard in the chest with his rifle, causing him to fall backwards.

"It's in my luggage in Rush. I can bring it to you." Thomas appeared most helpful, but didn't fool David. He knew Thomas would turn on him at the earliest opportunity.

"No, I'll find it myself. You won't need it." David kicked Thomas and, as if to prove David's point, Thomas tried to grab his ankle and pitch him over, but the Scot swatted Thomas on the side of his head with his gun and wrenched his leg free. The swindler collapsed, groaning.

"What do I do with you?"

Thomas paled, thinking he meant, *"How will I kill you?"*

David faced a genuine dilemma. He hadn't needed Buck's warning. *I can't shoot Thomas in cold blood, although, Lord knows, he deserves it. It's just not in my makeup. So, what to do?* His mind returned to the last bunch of lowlifes he had encountered. *"Of course."* he remembered. *In New York, the women made the Lederbeiters disrobe and booted them onto the street. I wonder how Thomas will fare in his underwear in the woods.*

"Stand up, you cretin. Stand up!" David prodded Thomas's ribs. "Take off your clothes. You heard me, strip. I want you in underclothes or so help me...." He brandished the gun towards the cliff.

Thomas got the message and peeled down to his skivvies.

"Give me your wallet!" Thomas passed it to David, who extracted the hundred dollars. "Ninety's going to the buckboard owner. You can have the rest...and your shoes. Throw your clothing into the river. Quickly!" David prodded with the Winchester again.

Thomas protested, but a dig with the gun barrel convinced him to comply.

"Baron Tookov." David said with a sneer. "I'm taking this," David hoisted the saddlebags, "to repay your investors. You're lucky, you've ten dollars. They lost everything. And don't even think of coming back to civilization, I'll make sure Buck Hall and the Pinkertons stay on the lookout for you." David took a deep breath. "Right, keep going south, Tookov. If you come back to Rush, you'll regret it."

"But ...!"

"No use appealing to my better side; I don't have one. Get the hell out of my sight before I change my mind."

Thomas turned and slumped away up the road to nowhere. He wasn't to know this was a dead end. He'd need a week to find the played-out mine. He'd be much thinner when he got there. Providing the bears hadn't eaten him. Or the cougars. The mosquitoes certainly would.

Chapter 39

Tam opened his eyes after his late afternoon nap, expecting to enjoy Marthe's beautiful face. Instead, it was his friend who stood there grinning like a Cheshire cat. "David!"

"Hello, old man. How are you?"

"I'm fine, I think. Sore, and weaker than I'd wish, but I'll be ready to go in a couple of days. What news do you have? Did you catch Thomas? You're filthy. And what's that smell?"

The young Scot laughed, "Yes, I did And yes, I'm filthy and yes, I smell something fierce! But it was worthwhile. I caught that crook Thomas..." David gave his friend a recap of his trip. "We've been more successful than I could ever imagine." He waved the mucky saddlebags to prove his point.

"Damn, I wish I'd seen him in his underwear in the middle of the forest. Serves him right. And Buck's advice was true; I'm glad you let Thomas live." Tam's focus shifted to his thousand-yard stare.

"It's all too easy to kill someone." He shook himself. "What happens next, Sir David?"

"I've to decide what to do with the mine. I'm meeting with John Williams; he's the mining engineer from last night. I'll pump him for information and that'll help me settle my mind. In the meantime, I need a bath."

"I agree, you stink!"

David ignored the jibe. "Are you being well nursed? Is there anything I can get you?"

On cue, Marthe appeared carrying a bowl of hot, soapy water, a brush and a razor.

"Thank you, David, but Marthe's doing a splendid job of supplying everything I need." The two smiled at each other. David recognized a conspiracy.

"Are you eating? Can I send dinner round from the hotel?"

The nurse answered. "Doctor Matheson prefers to keep him on a light diet, Sir David. Soon he'll be healthy enough to appreciate a full meal, but not today." Her low, throaty voice suited her exotic complexion.

"Good luck with Mr. Williams, David."

"Thanks Tam. Until morning, then. Take care of him, Marthe."

"Oh, I will, Sir David, that I will." Another secret glance between patient and nurse. David experienced a stab of jealousy as he left.

*   *   *

Marthe fussed around Tam's bed, plumping and straightening, unwilling to leave. The old soldier watched her, letting his thoughts roam. *I've been wounded before and been nursed before, so why does this woman have such an effect on me?* His eyes followed her to the window where she straightened an already straight curtain. *Mmmh, nice shape! Focus, Tam, focus! We've only known each other for a day, but I'm more awake with her than with anyone I remember.* He chuckled at the irony; he was feeling more alive, although last night he had been inches from death.

Marthe's so comfortable to talk with. We can discuss anything. I'm happy when she's in the room and I can't wait for her to return when she leaves. She has a way about her that brings me peace. And what a glorious smile! What the hell's going on? We haven't even been to bed yet! This, naturally, set Tam off on thoughts which kept his mind fully-occupied until he fell into a deep sleep.

Chapter 40

David's next stop was at the pool room where he brought Buck up to date...Buck and a dozen hangers-on, that is. "Buck, I need two of your men with me at all times, and I mean all. Your usual exorbitant rates, ok?"

The bandit nodded. His outfit hadn't been this busy or this flush for months.

David continued. "The bank one block over, does it have a safe?"

The Raider pulled a long face. "Yes, Sir David, it does. And a solid one. Why, a bunch of bushwhackers tried to blow it six weeks ago and didn't even dent it."

Based on the sideway glances exchanged among Buck's boys, the Scot had a good idea of who the failed safecrackers were.

"Thanks, Buck. I'll go there first, then to my room to change. I plan on returning later; the drinks are on me!" Nothing cheers up a bar like a generous patron.

*   *   *

David's bath was perfect: long, steamy and quiet. The immersions in the creek had left silt in places that hadn't seen the light of day since he was a baby in Ballboyne. The peaceful surroundings spurred him to consider his next steps. He sorted possibilities into probabilities, hopes into plans and came up with a blueprint that would depend on his conversation with Engineer Williams. With a strategy in place, he relaxed. The combination of the heat and the release of tension snuck up on him, and he dozed in the tub until the cooled water roused him. *Right. Enough lollygagging. Back to the pool hall.*

Chapter 41

John Williams' eyes lit up when he spotted the young noble pushing open the flap of the pool hall tent. "Sir David, Sir David, over here!" Buck and his boys clamored for his attention as well; free booze made David the most popular person in the county. Buck's Raiders had doubled in number since David's promise to buy.

"I'll be with you in a minute, Mr. Williams. Miss Betty, drinks for everyone!" The deafening cheers suggested this was a rare happening.

He rejoined the engineer. After the usual pleasantries, the Scot focused on business. "Sir, I need a crash course on mining. Educate me!"

Williams launched into an hour-long lecture on mining in general, mining zinc in Rush and mine finances. David was a sponge, soaking up knowledge, asking pertinent questions, filing it all away. To his surprise, he found this exciting. He hadn't expected to be so alive and engaged. He took stock of the Welshman. *His mining knowledge seems phenomenal. But what of his character? Is he a man I can trust?*

"Mr. Williams, I'm going outside to think for a moment. It's all right." David forestalled his protests. "Two of Buck's men will follow me. We'll talk more when I return. It will take only a few minutes."

The young Scot stepped out into the sweet night air, the evening birdcalls competing with the murmur of the nearby Buffalo River. The Raiders came along in tow, rifles under their arms. He compared the plan he'd developed in his bath against the information he'd learned from the engineer, checked it three ways from Sunday, and came to a decision. Turning on his heel, he went back to the bar and motioned for the Welshman to come and sit with him in the cool of the evening.

"I want to meet with the Morning Star owner tomorrow. Here's what we'll do." David spoke at length. The engineer's eyebrows shot up and down like semaphore flags, alternating from delight to determination. When David finished, the Welshman did everything but burst into song. He nearly jumped off the bench but David grabbed his arm. "No one, and I mean no one, must know. You can't even tell your wife. This has to be a complete surprise for Chase."

"Oh, Sir David, that'll be hard. I've been such a sourpuss since I was fired, and now I'm fair elated. She'll spot the difference in me at once, won't she?" Williams grinned. "I'll think of something." His eyes flicked to the pub's entrance. "Watch out, sir, here comes the Morning Star's foreman. Evenin', Bill."

Big Bill Brown appeared sober, dressed in his work clothes, his hatchet face split by a huge handlebar mustache. "Evenin', John. Sorry to hear Mr. Chase gave you the heave ho. I don't agree, but he's the boss." Bill's shifted his scrutiny to the Scot. "Sir David, is it?"

"Yes, that's me. How can I help you?"

"My boss wants to talk to you. Nine o'clock tomorrow morning. Can you find his office?"

"I could, but no matter. I can't see him at that time. Tell him I am available at one at the hotel."

The foreman had turned away, but David's reply spun him around.

"What are you saying, 'you can't see him'? You know who I'm talkin' about, right?"

"Certainly. Stanley Chase, owner of the Morning Star. I look forward to meeting him... tomorrow afternoon." David sensed his engineer slumping lower on the bench beside him.

Bill was at a loss. One didn't refuse a demand from Mr. Chase. He hemmed and hawed before grunting a begrudging, "We'll see." He glared at David, turned and started a slow walk to the mine, no doubt wondering whether the owner would shoot the messenger.

The mining engineer stared at the young man as though he had two heads. "Nobody turns down Mr. Chase around here. I hope you know what you're doing."

David smiled, thinking, *I hope so too.*

Chapter 42

One o'clock the next afternoon found David and John Williams waiting in David's room. No Chase. 1:05. 1:10. Still no Chase. Williams was pacing the floor by now. David smiled at the games grown men play. He had won the location, but Chase was dictating the time. At 1:15 on the dot, a fist rapped on the door. David opened it and ushered in his mining neighbor.

"Sir David." An economical response, devoid of emotion, until he noticed John Williams in the room. "Williams, what are you doing here?!"

"Ah yes, you're acquainted with my chief mining engineer, of course."

"I beg your pardon. Your what?"

"My chief engineer. I couldn't believe my good fortune when I heard he was available. Knowledge of the geology, etcetera. Most fortuitous." David realized he was sounding like Thomas Senior and shut his mouth.

Chase took the offered seat and sat like a black sphinx, assimilating and processing these added facts. *Sir David must know the richest vein runs through his mine. By now he'll have a rough idea of its value. Williams will have told him how anxious I am to buy it. Damn it to hell! I'll have to pay top dollar.* He marshaled his thoughts and adjusted his bargaining strategy. As a talented card player, he knew when to cut his losses. *The bottom line is, I need the mine and its ore. How do I get it and how much will it cost me?*

"Sir David, I hear you purport to be the owner of the Evening Star mine. Can you prove it?" Chase's question was on the brink of rudeness, but David ignored the implication.

"Of course, sir. Here you are." He nodded to Williams who handed over the ownership documents, including the certified letter from Broderick. Chase scrutinized them with care. David watched his face for a reaction, but little came from the master poker player.

"These appear to be in order. Perhaps you can share with me how you came to be the proprietor? You are, after all, the second supposed principal of the mine to appear within the past week."

"I understand, Mr. Chase. You ran into Baron Pyotr Tookov, whose real name is Peter Thomas." David told Chase of the scam Thomas had run to snare David's father, how David had bought the property from his father to make it easier for David to recover the family's investment and how he had tracked Thomas to Rush.

"And where is Thomas now?"

"He's no longer involved in this matter."

"Permanently?"

"He's alive, if that's what you mean, but he won't be coming back this way."

Damn. thought Chase. *If this upstart had killed Thomas, I might have had leverage over him.*

"What now, Sir David?"

"Mr. Chase, you called this meeting. So, let me ask you. What now?"

David's tactics impressed Stanley Chase. *This young man's a strong opponent.* "What are your plans for the mine?"

"I have no set plans. But I do have options. Selling the property is a possibility. That's the quickest way to recoup my investment." David avoided mentioning the money and bearer bonds he'd recovered from Tookov/Thomas. "Or I could re-open the mine. Mr. Williams favors this approach."

David saw Chase's involuntary blink. *He doesn't want my mine competing with the Morning Star. Good.*

"If you sell, will you give me the right of first refusal?"

"And why should I do that, sir?"

Chase blinked again. *Damn this little whippersnapper. Who does he think he is?* He swallowed his irritation. "I know the land, I know the mine, I know where the ore is."

"As does Mr. Williams. He knows precisely where the ore is. Especially on my side of our boundary." David didn't think it harmful to remind Chase he'd been poaching. "What offer are you prepared to put on the table? Please make your best offer and I'll get my engineer to evaluate it." *No harm in reminding Chase an expert will examine his submission.*

Silence again as Chase weighed his options. *I can't start with a lowball figure because Williams will recognize it as such. This upstart Rennie might walk out and find another buyer. There are plenty of companies interested, and Williams knows them. Dadgummit! If I'd kept Williams on the payroll for another two days, none of this would be happening. OK, I'd better make a decent offer, leave myself some wriggle room but not much, say, twenty percent.*

"Very well, for one hundred percent of the Evening Star, including its mineral rights, I'm prepared to offer $920,000."

"Is $920,000 your final offer, Mr. Chase?"

"Yes."

"All right, if you meet me here same time tomorrow, I'll tell you if you're the successful bidder."

Chase exploded. "What do you mean, 'the successful bidder'? You didn't tell me this was an auction!"

"If I had, would it have changed your bid? You told me this offer was your best."

The interchange flabbergasted Chase, a most rare and uncomfortable feeling for him.

"Do you want to reconsider your bid?" David was trying hard to hide his enjoyment. He brandished a sheaf of papers. "I have other offers in hand." Chase didn't realize the papers were a random sampling of prospectuses gathered from a table in the lobby of Chase's own hotel.

Chase blustered and huffed, but finally got control of himself. "Yes, I do." He fell silent while he did the math. "My best and final offer is one million, two hundred thousand dollars."

"Excellent, Mr. Chase." The two principals shook hands on the deal. "I'll let you know tomorrow. Please join me here at two." David ushered Chase to the exit. "Thank you for coming. Good day."

David closed the door behind Chase, eyed Williams, who was practically bouncing out of his skin, and held a finger to his lips. He waited for fifteen seconds, then snatched the door open. Sure enough, there was Bill the foreman listening on the other side. He gave David a dirty look, then hustled to catch up with Chase.

*   *   *

The partners spent the rest of the afternoon discussing the mine and its operation. Near six in the evening, they figured they had covered everything for the next day's meeting. "It'll be tougher tomorrow, Mr. Williams, because Chase'll be prepared. We caught him off guard today. We need to wait to see how he reacts to our proposal. Good bye, Mr. Williams. Remember, not a word to anyone."

"Peggy's fair bursting to find out what I'm up to, but she won't get a cheep out of me. She's just happy I'm engaged in something. Good day, Sir David."

Chapter 43

After breakfast next morning, David visited Tam and found him sitting in a wicker chair.

"Tam! You're out of bed!"

"I'm upright, at least. Marthe helped me over here. I'm still damned weak, but I'll be fine soon." At the mention of her name, his nurse came in and laid a proprietary hand on Tam's shoulder, intriguing David. The former soldier didn't allow public displays of affection. *Is he softening in his old age?*

"Thank you for taking care of my friend. He appears to be responding to your care." Marthe dipped a curtsy. "I'd like to talk to him. Do you mind...?"

"Not at all, Sir David. Please remember, he mustn't become excited or tired." She left the friends facing each other in comfortable chairs.

"Tam, me lad, a bullet hole aside, our venture is turning out to be wildly successful." David's smile robbed his comment of its seriousness.

His friend smiled back. "You might think differently if Buck had perforated your best shirt."

"You make an excellent point, Tam." The duo laughed, at ease with each other. "Now, John Williams and I meet with Chase this afternoon, but before we do, I want to raise a topic with you. Chase thinks I've two options: sell my mine, lock, stock and barrel; or re-open and work it. But there's a third choice, and it involves you." He spent an hour explaining himself.

Tam's reaction was lukewarm at first, then more interested. When his protege laid out his final idea, Tam offered his wholehearted support. "David, I'm always at your command, but in this instance, your command and my wishes dovetail." He shot a glance to the last place he had seen his nurse. "This'll work."

Stanley Chase didn't keep the young Scot and the engineer waiting. He arrived as two chimed on the clock downstairs, no game playing on the agenda. He was aware of his weaker position.

"Good of you to come, sir. Please take a seat. Can I get you anything?" David waved to the coffee on the side bar.

"No thanks, Sir David. I'd prefer to talk business."

"Excellent, I agree." The three sat around a small table. "Let's confirm our conversation of yesterday afternoon. We were discussing you buying the Evening Star for 1.2 million dollars. Is that correct?"

"Yes." Economical, unwilling to give away too much.

"I can't do that, I regret to say."

Chase sucked in his breath and held it. Again, the invisible wheels turned. He asked. "May I ask what the successful bid was?"

"Oh, yours was the highest. However, I've decided not to go through with the sale. Not all of it, anyhow."

A freight car full of pins could have dropped and nobody would have noticed.

"I don't understand."

"My apologies, sir, I'm not handling this well."

"*Yes, like a fox!*" thought his Welshman.

David continued. "Instead of putting all of my property on the market, I plan on selling a third of it, use the money for capital and work the mine. If you still wish to access the Evening Star's lode, I'll let you have thirty-three percent for four hundred thousand dollars, or one third of yesterday's offer." He knew when to stop talking.

Chase's silence was deafening. It was obvious the permutations and possibilities were being weighed, analyzed and filed or discarded. "Who will manage your mine, Sir David?" Chase glanced over at the engineer, which answered his own question. "Mr. Williams, of course. And the miners: who'll run them? Ah, your capable friend, McKenzie. Is he willing? He started off on the right foot. The town's buzzing with his exploits in the pool hall the other night. I understand his wound is on the mend. Bit of a rolling stone though, isn't he?"

"My friend's healing fine, thank you." *And he's planting roots for the first time in his life, thanks to Marthe!* "He's very willing. I'm more than happy with my partners."

"Partners?" The potential buyer shook his head in disbelief.

"That's right, I plan on keeping the majority ownership but I'd want Tam and Mr. Williams to enjoy their labors too. Your knowledge and working capital will complement this arrangement."

Chase chewed his lip. He hadn't suffered so many surprises in so short a period since... well, ever. The "auction", (although he wasn't sure there had been one), the minority share, the identity of the partners... it was a lot to assimilate. But his ordered mind sorted it out. *Leaving aside everything else, I have to access that vein and a third is better than none. Four hundred thousand dollars is a fair price and will leave my capital intact, plus I'll benefit from the engineer's expertise. On the downside, I need to watch myself, strict adherence to the rules. Mmmh. Sounds good.*

"Very well, Sir David, the Morning Star will buy a third of your property for four hundred thousand dollars." He extended his hand to shake on their agreement, remembered the tale of Tam and the injured Quantrill boys, and took it back.

David grinned at his discomfort. "Don't worry. I won't break your arm... today!"

Chapter 44

*H*ow many boats have I been on this past month? David straightened up from the rail and took another turn around the ferryboat's deck, monitoring the San Francisco skyline as he did so. *The Amador* had left the safety of the Oakland Mole behind and its sidewheel paddles were propelling it all too slowly across the bay to his Bella. *And how many trains? What a rail system they have here in America. Yet they travel at half the speed of the trains in Britain. And laying the rails through the mountains. The Rockies, was it? What a feat!*

The sun was cool on this morning and the keen breeze out of the north kept David moving as he reminisced over his recent travels. His circuit of the wee deck faced him towards San Francisco again. *Ah, where are you, my love, where are you? Come on, ferry. Hurry!*

*   *   *

David checked the address. 305 Ames Street in the Mission District, a wee wooden row house with fresh paint, roses and asters. He had walked to the home of Bella's uncle from the docks. Walked? Ran, almost. He couldn't wait to be with Bella again. He longed to see her smile, and to hold her in his arms. Yet he hesitated still. His youthful diffidence crept into his mind. *What if she's changed her mind? What if she's found someone else? What if she doesn't even remember me?! David, David, get a hold of yourself. She'll remember you, that much is for certain. Whether she loves you is a different matter, and there's only one way to find out. Knock on the damned door!* David smiled, hearing Tam in his thoughts.

David took a deep breath, lifted the brass knocker, banged it twice and stepped away. He heard a person shuffling to the entryway, a tired person's shuffle, and a fresh fear surfaced. *Who's this old person? Bella's ma isn't ancient, who...* and the door cracked open a notch to show an elderly woman he didn't recognize.

"Pardon me, Ma'am."

"May I help you?" A thick accent, Italian by the sound of it.

"I'm looking for Bella Gordon. Does she live here?"

"Bella Gordon? Are you the person who's been sending *lettere* to her?" The cottage door was still partly closed, but the woman's voice carried a spark of interest.

"Why, yes, I wrote them. May I ask your name, Ma'am?"

"Signora D'Aliesio, Signore."

"How do you know of the letters, Signora D'Aliesio? She lives here, then?" David's tone showed his stress.

"No, Signore, she never has." The old woman opened the entrance wide, curiosity in her eyes. "You've written often, haven't you?"

"I have, Ma'am, every day."

"Son, perhaps you've been sending them to the wrong house. Nobody called Gordon lives here."

The young Scot's shoulders slumped, disappointment writ large across his face. Tam's training kicked in anew: *Never surrender.*

"Your neighbors, Signora? Any of them a Scottish family? A bonny seventeen-year-old girl with a tall, skinny father, a short mother. Her brother's a tall, strongly-built fellow with red hair?" He knew he sounded desperate.

"No, I haven't seen any family that fits that description around here." The woman combed her memory. "But, uno momento, I heard of a big man living two blocks that way." She nodded to her right. "My granddaughter was telling me. She was quite taken with him!"

"Can I speak to your granddaughter, Ma'am?"

"She's at work. She only visits me on occasion."

David quizzed her more, but learned nothing new. He was turning to leave when the elderly lady spoke again. "Wait!" and retreated into her home. She returned minutes later with a bundle of envelopes tied with a red ribbon. "Here are your letters!"

"You still have them?!"

"Call me a romantic fool, but I knew they were love letters, and I hoped Miss Gordon would call for them one day." She passed the bundle to David. "Good luck, Signore!"

"*Grazie, Signora, graziemille!*"

*   *   *

David squared his shoulders and strode on with purpose. "I'll beat on every cursed door if need be to find that man. I hope it was George." But there was George, larger than life, copper hair ablaze, entering a garden gate at the far end of the next block.

"George! George!" George disappeared into another tidy row house. David raced there and knocked hard, eager to question Bella's brother.

It wasn't George who opened the door, it was Bella. His Bella, Bella of the raven tresses and flashing eyes... but at this moment the flash was recognition, then anger. "You! You promised to write!" She reared back, punched him hard in the face and slammed her uncle's door.

David found himself sitting on the ground with blood streaming from his nose. He staggered to his feet, reeled to the other side of the road and sat against a fence, head thrown back, staunching the flow. He tried to make sense of what had just happened but gave up, deciding he'd never understand women. In my wildest dreams, I never expected this! Now what?

After several minutes passed, George came out. When he spotted David, he crossed the roadway.

David groaned. He was in no mood or condition for a fight with someone of George's size. To his relief, George squatted beside him.

"Sir David?"

"Hello, George."

"Sir David, what happened? You never wrote as you promised, my sister's been pining away to a shadow and then you show up all unexpected like. How dare you hurt her!"

"Oh, George, 'The best laid plans of mice and men.' I've written dozens of times to Bella, telling her where I was and what I've been up to, but I had the wrong address. Here! Look!" David shoved the letters into George's hand.

"You sent them to 305, our home is 503! Well damn me!" George worked on the implications. "You didnae abandon her after all. Wait here while I talk to Bella."

A long ten minutes passed before George returned. "You'd better come in, Sire. But watch yerself, she's still mad at you. She was holding a paring knife when I left her."

Bella sat with her parents around the kitchen table. Bella had been weeping but had replaced the knife with his letters, much to David's relief. She avoided David's gaze, staring at the envelopes, turning them over and over in her hands. Fiona's motherly countenance was stern, but her eyes gave away the hope in her heart. Father Harry was out of his depth, trying to fathom the unfathomable.

"Bella, my dearie," David began. She shot him a hard glare. "Please, read the letter on the top."

She pulled the first envelope from the bundle, slit it open with the knife and pulled the sheets of cream writing paper onto the tablecloth. The lass hadn't read half the first page when her lips trembled and the tears flowed. She turned to page two.

"David!" Her voice broke as she jumped up and raced across the floor into his arms.

"Where have you been? What happened to you?!"

"Ah, now there's a story!"

Part 2

"For a' that and a' that
A man's a man for a' that"

"For a' that and a' that."
Robert Burns

Chapter 45

On January 2nd, 1906, David and Bella could be found at the Cliff House Restaurant where they dined while enjoying the spectacular view of the wild Pacific Ocean. Next, they visited the gem exhibit and the young Scot thought it an opportune time for his love to see another precious stone. He escorted her onto the Observation Tower overlooking the beaches and adopted the classic position of a suitor, down on one knee, hand outstretched, an open jewel box in his palm. The diamond wasn't overly big, but was of the finest quality. David had spent weeks hunting for the honey-colored cairngorm gems to set off the main attraction's brilliance. Finally, he'd located a brooch with a large central cairngorm in a pawnshop and persuaded a jeweler to cut it into a supporting cast of tiny teardrops.

Bella also was in a classical pose, that of the about-to-be-engaged woman. Her eyes were wide open in shock, her hands to her face, a sob away from a flood of tears.

"David, your proposal honors me beyond words..." In her hesitation, her beau jumped into the pause.

"I sense a 'but' coming."

Blast him, why did he have to be so gentle and understanding, and why did he have to be so lovable? "You're right, as usual, my dear. But... I can't, I won't marry you." She forestalled his protest by caressing his lips with a fingertip. "You know what I think of nobility marrying below their station. The union has never lasted. Dalliances? Yes, for a spell, but marriage? Never. We've discussed this for months, ever since you arrived in San Francisco. You understand how I feel." Her eyes bored into his, looking for acceptance, if not agreement.

"What of Lady Forsyth, my cousin? She married into a lower class..."

Bella didn't give him a chance to finish. "That's my point! You call me 'lower class', even you! What will the rest of your 'upper class' call me?" She stifled a sob. "I'll never forget your heroics on my behalf. And I'll never forget you." She took a long last look at her knight in shining armor. "Please, don't call on me again."

Bella rushed to David's carriage and told the driver, an old friend by now, to take her home. The floodgates opened, and she wept wildly.

David was stunned. *I don't understand. I'm certain of our love. We've expressed it in word and touch, despite being chaperoned by a relative. And we debated at length the differences in our upbringing and station in life.* David shook his head. *I've tried to convince her that I've abandoned the trappings and responsibilities of noble birth, but Bella obviously doesn't agree.*

He sighed in disappointment, then became exasperated. *I shouldn't have made her commit by proposing but I was so frustrated with her hesitancy. What a damned fool I was! She committed, finally, but in the wrong way. Well, to hell with her! To hell with them all!*

His anger boiled over and he left the restaurant in high dudgeon, slamming doors, kicking cats, cursing kids, blaming everyone but himself for his feeling of failure.

Chapter 46

Bella's journey home lasted beyond an hour. She brooded once more over her abrupt change of heart; from wanting to share her life with David, to firmly rejecting that future.

It was Ailene Dunne, the Irish scullery maid's fault. Madame Patrice employed both she and Bella, housing them on the top floor. One recent evening, the lasses had arrived at the doors to their rooms at the same time and started chatting...

"Are ya' finished for the day then, Bella?"

"Aye, Ailene, the bairns are asleep so I'm free till the morn. How about you?"

"Much the same, but I've to be up early. Hey, do you want to join me for a drink?" Ailene gestured to the door of her room.

Bella didn't drink much, but the thought of adult company enticed her. "I'd like that, thank you. A little one for me, please. I'm not much of a drinker."

"I can make up for that!" Sure enough, she poured a finger of Irish whiskey for Bella and four for herself.

Ailene's room looked smaller than Bella's because of the clutter. Her clothes were strewn here and there and matched Ailene's appearance, scruffy, messy and jumbled. Her unkempt and stringy hair straggled out from under her not-quite-clean white kitchen cap, which matched her not-quite-clean apron. She appeared pudgy, pale and bowed with age, although Bella knew her to be only four years older than herself.

The evening passed, the whiskey flowed, tongues loosened, secrets revealed themselves.

"Have ya' got a man in your life then?" Ailene wasn't backward at coming forward.

"Yes, I do, a very special man. He's not only good and handsome and kind, but he saved my honor twice when I immigrated."

"Oh, do tell! Details please!"

Though Bella had drunk little whiskey, it had loosened her tongue. She described in great detail how she and David had met, how David had saved her on the ship, how David had rescued her from the

Lederbeiters brothel, how David... how David... how David...!

Ailene laughed and threw up her hands in surrender. "Stop, woman, you make him sound like a saint!" She downed her drink and re-filled the glass. Bella refused a top-up. "What does your man do for a living, anyhow?"

"He's nobility and doesn't... "

Ailene jumped off the bed. "Nobility! Oh, you puir misguided fool! Nobility! It's not your heart he's interested in, it's your knickers!"

Ailene was screaming now, spittle flecking her mouth, her eyes bulging with venom and rage. Her anger stunned Bella who jolted back into her chair, raising her arms in defense. But, as quickly as Ailene had erupted, she collapsed onto her bed and curled into a ball, wailing in terrible agony.

Bella being Bella, she moved to comfort her erstwhile attacker. "What's wrong, Ailene? What's the matter with you?" She sat beside Ailene and stroked her hair, whispering words of encouragement. A thought struck her. "Is it nobility you're mad at?" Echoes of her family's warnings jumped from their temporary hiding place.

It took a while, but Ailene calmed enough to hear Bella's support. She dried her tears and turned to her attic neighbor.

"Oh, Bella, I'm sorry I shouted at you, but I see you following the same slippery path that I did... and I wouldn't wish that on anyone."

"What do you mean, dearie? What path is that?"

Ailene sighed and took a deep pull on her drink. "Jasus, Mary and Joseph, if I don't tell someone, I'll burst, for sure." She crawled through the cobwebs of her memories, examining, discarding or putting them aside for the telling.

She continued her tale, her voice barely rising to a whisper. "When I was fifteen, I worked as a scullery maid at Castle... no, I won't name names. Let's just say it's a prominent family in County Donegal. I was young, pretty, and really, really stupid."

"Stupid? How so?"

"Hear me out, you'll see. The family had twin sons, Declan and Seamus, they were five years older than me and always professing their love. Of course, I knew they just wanted into my bed. Declan, the older twin by an hour, had a cruel streak so I never let my guard down around him, but Seamus acted sweet and gentle and said he wanted to marry me. I began to believe him and to love him."

She took another swig of whiskey.

"Is that what you meant by 'stupid'?

"Yes and no. There's worse to come." She hiccupped, then sobbed again. "Bear with me, Bella, you're the only person I've told." She hugged her pillow to her chest. "One night, Declan was in his cups and caught me in the root cellar. He tore at my clothes and thrashed me when I resisted."

She started yowling again, a high-pitched constant wail. The keening set Bella's nerves further on edge as she relived the memories of her own assaults on the steamship from Scotland.

"What happened next, Ailene?"

"I shouted for help but the more I screamed, the more Declan beat me. I was fearing the worst when his younger brother found us and, supposedly, rescued me."

"What do you mean, 'supposedly'?"

Ailene's voice hardened, rising in pitch and volume. "BECAUSE IT WAS A SET UP!"

"A set up? I don't understand."

The Irish lass crumpled in tears, sobbing so hard that it seemed she was wrenching her very soul.

"I discovered later that the twins had tossed a coin to decide who'd attack me and who'd rescue me. Seamus won. They figured I'd be so grateful to the rescuer, it'd be easy to seduce me... and they were right."

"You mean...?"

"Yes, I gave in to Seamus' advance, fool that I was. And you know what? After the first time, I discovered I loved it and couldn't get enough and Seamus naturally obliged."

"And then what?"

"We slept together every night for a month, Seamus declaring his undying love. But he told me his parents wouldn't let him marry me and we should elope to Dublin, almost two hundred miles from Donegal. We lodged at an inn and spent a heavenly week there..." Ailene broke down, but in anger, not in tears. "... Seamus left to get a newspaper... and never returned!"

Chapter 47

"**W**hat! He abandoned you? How could he!"

Ailene's voice escalated into a bitter diatribe. "It was part of their plan, Bella. Stage the attack, seduce the colleen, take her far from home so no message gets back to her family, enjoy her, then dump her. I wonder how many other young lasses they treated in the same way?"

Bella was astounded. "What happened next, how did you survive?"

"Seamus didn't pay the inn-keeper, his last 'gift' to me. I had no money. The landlord called the Garda, who put me in jail. When the Magistrate found out I'd been living with Seamus without the benefit of marriage, he sent me to the Magdalene Laundry."

"The Magdalene Laundry? What's that?"

Ailene exhaled. "This is difficult for me, Bella. It's what makes me a slave to the drink. Give me a moment, please." She ghosted a weak smile. "You're an excellent listener, lass." She refilled her glass and composed herself.

"The Magdalene Laundries are hell on earth." Ailene stared into the distance. "They're run by an order of Nuns whose supposed mission is to save and rehabilitate loose women."

"Loose women? But you weren't..."

"I know, but that's what they call anyone who fornicates outside the marriage bed. We're considered a danger to others: to women by being an example and to men by being a temptation. They held me prisoner there for three months until they found out I was pregnant."

Bella looked around the room for a child, but in vain. "Where... "

Ailene ignored her. "We had our heads shaved, put on bread and water diets, thrown into solitary confinement, even flogged. They gave me a new name, Penitent 3517. The nuns were expected to rehabilitate us by teaching needlework or embroidery but in reality, we worked in the laundry for 10 hours a day, making money for the Order."

Bella had no words; the story horrified her.

"After discovering my pregnancy, they beat me again, then took me to a home for unwed mothers. I hoped I'd be better cared for because of my condition, but that's not what happened. They still subjected me to beatings and abuse, and I still was their slave, washing and ironing clothes. I worked until the day I bore my child." Ailene wept in deep distress.

Bella thought she spied a chance to lighten Ailene's burden. "Tell me about your baby."

Ailene's voice changed to a flat, fearful monotone. She sat up, arms around her knees, rocking back and forth. "I can't. I never saw it. They took it from me as soon as it was born. I don't know if it was a boy or a girl... or if it lived."

Ailene had no tears left and telling her tale had exhausted her.

"There I am, stupid. Stupid for believing Seamus. Stupid for letting him into my bed. Stupid for going to Dublin with him." She grabbed Bella's shoulders, glared into her eyes and shook her hard. "Don't be as stupid as me! Don't let any nobility get between your legs! And don't believe a word he says about love!"

Bella hugged the young Irish lass, Ailene hugged her back, clung to her, never wishing to relinquish her grip. She was sobbing once more... why not, her heart had been broken again.

An hour went by, Ailene slept, Bella couldn't. She was comparing David with Seamus and Declan. *They can't be the same, David is sweet and gentle and... and that's exactly the words Ailene used to describe Seamus! But David wouldn't act like that, he's honest... except when he's not! He stole the valuables from the Lederbeiters,* don't forget. *Perhaps David's more like the twins than I care to admit.*

These seeds of doubt had found fertile ground in Bella's mind, undermining the love she felt, had felt, towards Sir David. In addition, her family's concerns about nobles marrying below their station had resurfaced, unbidden, toxic and debilitating.

Bella had came to a decision; she wouldn't marry David.

Chapter 48

Tam McKenzie woke to two great disadvantages. A Colt .45 was poking him in the ribs, and he was as naked as a plucked partridge.

"What the *HELL* are you doing in me bed with me wife!" An angry Irish brogue.

Make that three disadvantages. Wife! Marthe said she was a widow. What the hell indeed!

Tam glanced over at the aforementioned Marthe. She sat up, holding the sheet in front of her, shielding herself from the gaze of two men who had seen her womanly charms up close and personal. She smiled at the interloper, all coy like. *Smiling at him?* Tam had a sinking feeling this wasn't a case of mistaken identity, as he had first thought. *Uh oh, if I'm not careful, I'll get an arse whipping.* He eased himself upright.

"Stop right there, mister! Who are you, and what are you doing in me bed? Get out of there!" Tam chose the latter command and slowly complied, swinging his legs over the wooden frame. It's hard for a man to be aggressive or even assertive when he's buck naked and facing a .45. What does he do with his hands, for example?

"My name's Tam McKenzie, sir, and we have a simple case of miscommunication..."

"Miscomm...! Miscommunication! You've been communicating just fine with me woman." The gunman switched his attention to Marthe.

"Marthe, what do you have to say for yourself. Did he force himself on you?"

Marthe saw a chance to improve her reputation. "You might say that, Rory. He has been very forceful." People can interpret facts in many ways. "But you were away for seven years, Rory O'Connor! 1899, was it? Where were you?"

"We'll talk of that later. First off, I'll be teaching this villain a lesson" Rory looked as though he could. A decade south of the Scot's mid-forties, he was a wild, hard Irishman with a shock of red hair and a beard that could house a colony of swallows. Tam's six months in Rush allowed him to recognize a miner when he saw one. Rory had sinews and muscles of knotted steel, shoulders wide enough to yoke to a plough and thighs like a prize bull. His nose, broken so often as to be flat, testified to his enthusiasm for fighting, if not his ability.

"Sir! Rory! Do you really want Marthe to see such bloodshed?" The ex-soldier nodded in Marthe's direction, Rory's eyes followed and his gun followed his eyes. Tam lunged for the weapon and jerked it sideways. Rory got one shot off, which destroyed the cuckoo clock over the fireplace, before his foe could twist the Colt out of his grasp. Rory still wanted to attack so Tam gave him a love pat on the temple with the butt of the pistol, leaving Rory sitting on the floor, dazed and mumbling Irish curses.

Marthe rushed to the miner's side. "Rory, Rory, are you all right? Oh, I'm sorry that you came home to this. But it's been years without me seeing hide nor hair of you. I thought you had died. Please forgive me." Marthe began to wail, which sped up the Irishman's recovery and focused his mind on consoling her.

The Scottish nudist figured this was an excellent time to pull on his breeches. "Marthe, Rory might appreciate a whiskey. Go fetch him a glass. Ach, bring the bottle and three glasses." Marthe scurried over to the cupboard. "Sir, what Marthe says is true, she thought you dead, I thought you dead. Obviously, we were wrong. We three have some sorting out to do, but it needn't be at the end of a gun. Here." Tam handed the Colt back to Rory. And held his breath.

Rory didn't know what to do. *I had the upper hand, the bloke snatched it from me, then gave it back! I could just shoot him, but how do you shoot a man when he refused to kill you while he had the chance?* He was working that out when Marthe arrived with the whiskey and poured a good belt into each glass.

*   *   *

Two hours passed and Marthe was loudly asleep on the bed. Rory did his best to keep upright by flinging his arms tight around Tam's neck.

"You're the finest mate I've ever had, Tam! 'strue! You're a pal if ever there was one. Why do you have to leave? Have another drink. Marthe!" He waved the empty flask towards his wife, but releasing his grip on Tam was a mistake. He gradually, majestically slid down Tam's torso, waist, and legs until his head was resting on Tam's boots. Rory joined Marthe in a duet of snores. Tam moved Rory's head onto a pillow, slipped outside and sat on the porch while he figured out the rest of his life.

Chapter 49

A logical man, Tam sorted his options into the Possibles, the Impossibles, the Desirables and the I-wouldn't-touch-that-with-a-ten-foot-barge-poles.

It appears I'm no longer married, so it's fortunate Marthe and I lived common law. Truth be told, I was getting itchy feet anyhow. It hasn't been boring around here, but there's little to relieve the monotony. Being foreman at the mine has given me the greatest pleasure, reminds me of my army days, molding and shaping young, headstrong bucks into a team with a shared goal.

He took a pull on his pipe. *Rush isn't big enough for both Rory and me. When he wakes up, he'll have one heck of a hangover and remember who encouraged him in his drinking. And, more importantly, the situation with our wife will incense him and he'll try to exact revenge. OK, keep a lookout for trouble.*

Dawn was peering over the rim of the cliffs on the other side of the river and the camp was showing life, women lighting fires, kids hauling water, the smells of breakfasts wafting through the trees. The Scot sniffed the air. More change was coming.

*   *   *

Tam wasn't the sole early riser that morning. He heard the bustling footsteps before John Williams, the chief engineer, hove into view.

"Morning, John."

"Good morning, Tam." The sing-song Welsh accent made the standard greeting sound like a melody. "You're up already. Couldn't sleep?"

"You might say that." He sighed. His Scottish reserve left him reluctant to divulge too much to his partner. But he also knew rumor mongers. Their take on the events of last night would soon be public news. Not that he cared a whit but he had the reputation of the Evening Star to consider. "John, we need to talk. Are you free now?"

"Sorry, my friend, the assay results of that new vein are due this morning and I want to see them as soon as they arrive. If what I suspect is right, we'll be very rich men!" The engineer danced a jig in the middle of the road. Tam had to smile; Williams' Celtic enthusiasm was impossible to resist. "Can you tell me what's on your mind while we walk?"

"I need your undivided attention, John, so let's wait until you have your results. I'll bring you up to date then." *Good job Sir David's arriving back in Rush next week, we need to talk.*

Chapter 50

Tam enjoyed the warmth of the fine spring morning as he watched the steam engine chug into the Yellville depot. Several miners got off, a few trailing their families, all toting huge bundles of belongings. *Looks as though they're planning on staying here for a while. And why not? The mines here in Marion County are exploding with activity, thanks to our find of the new vein at the Evening Star. But where's David? His telegram from San Francisco said he'd be on this train and it's leaving. He also told me he's selling the mine! Why? What's happened since he left here three months ago? We need to talk.*

A drunk lurched out of the last door of the first carriage, tumbled down the steps and sprawled in the platform's dirt. He wasn't entirely out of it, though. He kept his bottle intact by holding it over his head. The porter threw two suitcases and a briefcase after him, the latter hitting him on his backside. Tam heard mutterings of "Lousy drunk!" and, more vehemently, "Lousy tipper!". He dismissed the display of alcohol surfeit and returned to looking for his young benefactor.

The engine pulled away, leaving only the drinker and the station agent/ticket collector/porter/chief dogsbody. *Where the heck is he? The schedule says this arrival is the only one today, but I'd better check.* Tam's chase after the agent took him close by the tippler, who waved a feeble arm and croaked "Tam!"

Should I know this sot? Maybe from a different bar in a different place at a different time? Wait, I recognize that jacket. It was much cleaner when I last saw it. "Who are you, sir?" The old soldier turned the bum on his back. "Good grief! Sir David?! Is that you? I don't believe it! Say something, please!"

His confusion was understandable. Here lying before him was a wreck of a man, a man who hadn't shaved, bathed or changed his clothes for weeks prior to his leaving San Francisco. It appeared he'd been drinking the entire time as well, based on the smell of his breath and his inability to stand. His hair was greasy and matted, his scraggly beard similarly disheveled, his eyes bloodshot and bleary.

"Tam..." his friend rolled onto his side and retched... and retched more. He lay there exhausted.

What the hell, David never drinks this much. Something serious must have happened. First things first. Sober him up and take him to Rush. He'll tell me what the problem is when he's able. One of the company wagons can handle the luggage.

"Okay, up onto your horse. Hang on, there, hang on! I don't want to tie you to your saddle. Grip the reins hard. I'll lead you for a while until you find your bearings."

David promptly toppled off and threw up again.

"Mmh, that won't work. Let's get water into you and a little food, then we'll try again."

David successfully drained half of Tam's canteen of pure spring water and nibbled two hardtack biscuits. Later that morning, his guide led him south towards Rush. It took the young Scot an hour before he could lift his eyes to enjoy his surroundings. The magnificent Ozark spring helped. Glorious redbuds and improbable dogwoods, resplendent in their creamy layers of flowers, embraced him. Warblers and wood ducks, pigeons and partridges, goldfinches, meadowlarks and quail added their melodic welcome to the slowly-recovering David.

"Tam, stop, that's enough torture for one day. I need to rest." They both slid off their horses. "Give me my bottle please."

"Certainly. Here, catch!" Tam tossed the whiskey flask just out of David's reach and watched with satisfaction as it evaded the young man's fingers, fell to the ground and shattered. The contents seeped into the earth, causing a colony of ants to bless their maker.

"What were you thinking, you daft gommerel! That was my last jug!" He tried to slug Tam, but his mentor wrapped him in a bear hug until that foolish notion passed. David struggled and shouted and glowered. Tam held tight, David's resistance lessening as he grew weaker. The older Scot grabbed his protege's chin and turned it to face him. "Look me in the eyes, David. We need to talk and talking through the end of a bottle won't help."

Tam kept David upright. "Speak to me, my friend, speak to me. I expect the telling will sober you. Can you do that?"

Finally, David relaxed. The ex-soldier released him, tied their mounts to a convenient alder and claimed suitable rocks as seats beside a sizable creek. Tam held his tongue; David would talk when ready.

Chapter 51

'Ready' was a long time coming, but Tam's patience outlasted David's reluctance.

"It's Bella…" David began. It was tough getting the words to form. He was angry… with her, for sure… but chiefly with himself. He was facing the endless highway of silent self-recrimination, but Tam pulled his focus back into the present.

"Go on, my friend. It concerns Bella…"

The silence invited the young Scot to fill it. Bit by bit, he spilled everything: the intense connection they had made, and how their months in San Francisco had deepened their love, or so he had thought. Then the lassie had withdrawn from him and into herself, causing him to hurry the issue by proposing.

"… she asked me not to call on her." His voice was a whisper now and he was near to tears.

"Is that when the drink grabbed you?"

David shook his head, cleansing the memories of Bella. "Not at first, Tam, not at first. The telegram from Williams telling me the value of the new vein spurred me into selling the Evening Star. I investigated and researched, talked to other owners about evaluating a mine and advertised that we'll be having the auction in Rush at the end of month." He raised a slight grin. "I was the most popular man in town for several weeks. I had more free dinners than I could count."

David's lightened mood evaporated. "Busying myself with the sale of the Evening Star kept me on the straight and narrow. I went off the deep end when I had too much free time." He lifted his bleary eyes and tried to look at the elder Scot, but his shame was overwhelming. "I don't remember everything. I know I made a fool of myself many, many times." Another gaze into the past. "I have a tattoo now!"

"What? A tattoo? Where? Is it visible?" Tam's voice rose as he scanned David's skin.

"Calm down, old man, calm down. It's a handsome set of Chinese characters. As for where, you'll never see it! I had it done in Chinatown... I think. An American in Chinatown? Maybe?"

The "old man" wasn't convinced. He paused for a moment before coming up with a plan to kill two birds with one stone. "Sire, let's take a walk along this creek. Look, there's a fisherman's path. The exercise will do you good."

David grumbled but recognized the benefit of a stroll. The ex-soldier picked up his saddle bags. pulled his friend upright and led the way.

"I'll bet there's nice trout in there." Tam pointed to a deep pool beside the track. It was six feet below the trail, under an overhang and shaded by alders.

David stopped, glad of the change of topic. "You're right. I'd try a black fly, a number 12 Adams Caddis..."

Tam pushed him into the pool.

An almighty splash cut off David's yell. He'd entered the water on his back and couldn't find his footing. He floundered around like a beached version of the trout he'd been envisioning, but surfaced at last, spluttering dire retributions on his erstwhile friend.

"What the hell, McKenzie! Why did you do that? Just wait till I get my hands on you...! Good grief, this water's as cold as an Eskimo's nose! Get me out of here!"

Tam rummaged in his bags and came up with a bar of soap from his "housewife", as soldiers called their shaving kit. "No such luck, laddie. You might as well have a bath while you're there. Heaven knows, you need scrubbing down." Keeping out of David's reach, he placed the soap on a rock near his protege, He was well aware of the young noble's evil intentions regarding his own dry state.

David groused and complained, but his heart wasn't in it. He recognized that he stank like the bottom of a parrot's cage. "What am I to wear, smarty? These are all the clothes I have with me."

"There are spares in my bag. They're big for you, but they'll do. Don't be such a sissy. Strip!"

His smelly companion swam to the soap, undressed and lathered himself.

"That's a handsome tattoo."

"What, you saw it? You saw it when I said you couldn't? How could you!"

"You bent over and there it was! How could I help seeing it?! What did the tattoo artist tell you it meant?"

David kept soaping himself. "'Good Fortune'. 'Happy Love' didn't fit."

Tam tried to suppress his laughter but failed. Soon he was grabbing at trees to avoid falling in the creek.

"What!"

His friend laughed harder. "'Good Fortune' huh?"

"Yes. So?!"

"Peking Duck."

"What do you mean, 'Peking Duck'?"

"The artist might have been trained in Chinese inking but he couldn't read Chinese worth a damn. Your tattoo reads 'Peking Duck'. He must have copied it off a menu from a Chinese restaurant."

David's confusion tiptoed across his face but his sense of humor finally showed up, until he was laughing too.

"Just my luck to have a friend who learned Mandarin while stationed in Hong Kong!" David climbed out of the creek and dried himself with Tam's spare shirt.

"Sir David. Now that you're abandoning the mining business, how do you plan to spend your days? Being a gentleman of leisure won't suit you."

"I've invested in the California timber industry. You'll remember my affinity for trees and lumber when I was growing up in Scotland?" Tam nodded. "I purchased a large tract of forest in north of San Francisco. That'll keep me occupied and out of mischief."

"Good heavens, David, first it was a tattoo, then a timber baron, what else have you been up to while out of my sight?" They laughed, comfortable in each other's company.

"Oh, I forgot to mention...I bought a house!"

Tam surrendered.

Chapter 52

"Mamma, what's wrong with Miss Bella?"

It was William Junior, the perceptive child, so well-attuned to the moods of others.

"Your tutor? What do you mean, Junior?" His mother, Madame Patrice Steben, was startled to hear her own thoughts expressed in her son's words. *From the mouths of babes.*

"She's changed. She's not as much fun anymore, and she never laughs. She's sad all the time."

"Really?" Mrs. Steben again secretly agreed with her son. "Katie, what do you think?"

The seven-year-old took her head out of the clouds long enough to reply. "It's as though she's in mourning. It must be boy trouble." *More from the mouths of babes.*

"Thank you, children. I've seen the difference in her too. She seems so forlorn. Do you remember how cheerful she was when she first came to work here and how much fun she made it to learn?" A chorus of agreements filled her ears. "William, do you recall hating sums?"

"I do, Mother, and now that's my favorite subject, thanks to Miss Bella. Papa's ever so happy with me."

"And Katie, she helped you find an interest beyond drawing, didn't she? What's the word she uses? I forget the English."

"Zoology, Mamma, animals. I'm going to be a horse doctor. Or a kitty doctor."

"Papa's pleased with you, too, *ma petite.*" Patrice turned the problem over in her mind. "What do you suggest? Should we keep her or should we bring back Ursula?"

"NOOOOO, Mamma! NOOOOO, please no! She was mean, and she smelled like Papa's brandy. Make Bella stay."

His sister added her remonstrations. "Ursula used to pull my hair and beat us with a switch. I hated her. If she comes back, I'll run away."

"All right, both of you, all right. Miss Gordon stays. She and I will talk. Let's see if we can help her get over her sadness. Any ideas?"

"We'll paint a card. I could write a poem for her."

"And I'll draw a kitty-cat. She'll love that."

"Splendid, children. Be extra nice to her and finish your homework. That will cheer her. I'll meet with her after lunch." Graceful as ever, Patrice rose from the loveseat and left.

Chapter 53

"Miss Gordon... Bella, please don't be nervous, but we have to talk." Employer and tutor sat in the conservatory overlooking the Japanese garden. The spring sun shone through the dissipating fog, warming the room to a pleasant temperature.

Bella relaxed just a smidgeon. Her job here as governess to the children was the only bright spot in her life nowadays and any suggestion of losing her post was unbearable. She'd found the position five months ago, soon after arriving in San Francisco, and loved it.

The transition from her uncle's home in the Mission District to this posh mansion on Nob Hill could have been difficult, but the Steben clan treated her as one of the family. Her Uncle Jack, bless him, had tried his best. He'd made the four Gordons very welcome, but the added relatives left his house crowded, not enough beds, not enough chairs, not enough space. Here, she had her own room and shared a bath with the other servants. Although in the attic, it was hers. For the first time, she had a place of her own.

The residence itself was wonderful, a three-story mansion built in the Queen Anne style. Madame told her it had twenty-eight rooms. Imagine, all those rooms for a family of four. Mr. Steben could afford it. After all, he was a significant shareholder and Director in the Southern Pacific Railroad Company. A tall, commanding gentleman with silver hair and a trimmed beard, he adored his wife and even his youngsters. This was in stark contrast to Bella's experience with the British aristocracy's approach to child-rearing where "children should be seen and not heard". Another reason why the lass enjoyed working here.

"I want you to know we've noticed the children's improvement since you've been with us. It's not only their improvements in reading and writing and counting, but also their desire to learn. They're more inquisitive." Patrice laughed. "Too many questions sometimes! But that's healthy, and we have you to thank for that. You bring light into their eyes and hearts and minds and I can't praise you sufficiently."

Bella relaxed a little more, only a little because she knew a 'but' was coming.

"I'm increasing your wages by a dollar a week. I won't have my neighbor enticing you to work for her."

Her young governess protested. "I'd never leave your employ, Ma'am." *Was I being lured away?* She replayed her recent conversations with the neighbor, Mrs. Atkinson. *Madame is correct. I was being courted.* "Thank you, Ma'am. I'm grateful to you for my position here and the increase in my wage. And don't worry, I would never tutor for your neighbor!" She was remembering the bruises on the Atkinson children's arms.

"Good. That's settled. Well, almost."

Here it comes.

"Before I raise your pay, I need to know what's happened to you." Patrice's gentle smile and concerned look robbed her comment of its seriousness. "Your *joie de vivre*, your spark has been missing and I want to see it return. So, tell me, is there something troubling you? Katie thinks it's boy trouble. Is she correct? Is there a boy in your life who's causing you pain?"

Bella was shocked. Was it so obvious that even a seven-year-old could recognize and name her torment? She recoiled, but Patrice leaned forward, taking her hand. "Sometimes all a person needs is to talk to a friend. Do you have a friend?"

Bella shook her head. She'd talked, even cried, to her Mum but had found that to be unsatisfying. Fiona was out of her depth. *Can I let this lovely woman into my heart? Maybe a glimpse of my misery might satisfy her.*

"Well, Madame, yes, there is a boy, a man..." Bella started haltingly.

"Go on, *ma cherie.*"

Piece by piece, Patrice drew Bella's story from her: the chance encounter with Sir David at the street party in Scotland; the pair ending up on the same ship coming to America; David twice saving her from the Lederbeiter clan; and how they'd had to part while he tended to family business in Arkansas. She shed many tears in the telling, but these stopped as she recounted her beau's appearance at her uncle's door. Her voice dropped to a whisper as she reminisced, her mind far off as she described the intense emotion she felt for her shining knight. The weeping started afresh when she related David's marriage proposal and her rejection of it, and of him.

"What happened, my dear? Why the shift from love and your intention to be with him always, to banishment? It sounds so... final."

"Oh, it's final, Madame. I never want to see him again. Well, I want to, but it's too painful. Oh, I'm all confused!"

"Help me understand. You won't marry him because..." The elegant woman's voice trailed away; her hazel eyes full of empathy for the young lass. She had Bella's hand in hers and was stroking it as if she were calming a kitten.

"Because he's nobility and I'm a tradesman's daughter. Marriages like that always fail, always. I've seen them back in Scotland and they all break down, and I don't want it to happen to us... to me. I've tried to block out the memories of the failures but I know I was only fooling myself. They never work." Bella was keening now, covering her face and rocking to and fro in anguish. Her conversation with Ailene hovered below the surface of her consciousness like a stick of dynamite. "How do I even know he loves me? Maybe he just wants under my skirts. Love me and leave me? How do I know?"

"Ah." Patrice understood at last. "You have two worries, does he truly want to marry you, and could such a marriage be a success. Am I right?"

Bella thought for a moment. "Yes, Madame, that's correct."

"Does he want to marry you?" Patrice turned the riddle over in her mind. "Or does he want you in his bed? Bella, when you were describing how you met David and how he saved you from harm on the voyage, it sounded as though you were sure of your love for each other."

"Yes, I was. I am. I was." Bella's confusion was evident.

"Did he press you to make love?"

"No, he was a perfect gentleman. I could tell he wanted to, as did I, but he restrained himself."

"What changed your thinking, then?"

The tutor kept Ailene's name secret but recounted the details of her recent chance meeting. Patrice was horrified by the tale of Irish nobility and laundries, but also saw a silver lining.

"Bella, I understand how this story must upset you, but let me ask my question again. You've known him for months. Has he pressed you to make love?"

"No, Madame. Never."

"There you have it. If he was a scoundrel, he would be pressuring you immediately after you met, like the twins you told me about. If he's waited this long, then I believe he is a gentleman and you have no worries on that score. Do you agree?"

"Yes, I think so, Ma'am." There was still doubt in Bella's voice. "You may be right, he is a decent man. But I still believe marriage between nobility and tradesmen's daughters are doomed to failure."

Patrice smiled. "What do you call it, class distinctions, *n'est-ce pas*? You fear you won't be able to fit into his world and he'll tire of you and drop you for someone who does. Is that correct?"

Bella stared at her. "Why, yes, you're right, on every count. How do you know that?"

Patrice rose from her seat and took a turn around the room, ending up looking into the distance, remembering her own history from not so long ago. She sighed and decided. "Bella, what I'm going to tell you must never leave this room, *comprenez-vous?* Never! Do you promise?"

"I do, Madame, of course." Bella came to the edge of her seat. It was her turn to search the other woman's eyes.

Patrice still hesitated. "This could ruin me if it ever got out."

Chapter 54

Patrice opened a silver box which graced the end table. She offered a cheroot to Bella, who declined, then selected one herself and lit it with a safety match. She inhaled deeply, held her breath, then let the smoke curl upwards from her nose and lips. She was still in serious thought but shook herself and spoke, holding her employee's eyes in a powerful gaze.

"I'm happily married, wouldn't you say?"

"Yes, Ma'am, it looks that way to me."

"And I'm married to William, a man of standing in this city, a respected businessman whose opinion is sought on many topics. In other words, he has status as well as wealth. Agreed?"

The lassie couldn't fathom where this was going, but again agreed.

"It makes sense, then, that he would wed someone supportive of his endeavors, someone who is his equal and will fit comfortably into his society. Do you concur?"

"I do, Madame, But what..."

Her employer shushed her. "Bear with me for a second longer, *ma cherie*." She took another pull on her cheroot. "Do you think I qualify, Bella?"

"Why of course. You're the epitome of the supportive wife, mother and hostess. You're greatly admired for the ease with which you carry out the duties required by your husband's position."

"Thank you for your honesty, or maybe flattery. But no matter. I've done well, then... for a cabaret dancer!"

Bella's surprise was evident in her stutter. "I... I... I don't understand. What do you mean, cabaret dancer?"

"Just that, I danced at the Moulin Rouge in Paris. An exclusive cabaret, for sure, but nevertheless, it's still a cabaret. That's where I met William. His father had sent him to Europe after college to broaden his horizons and to make contacts. As it turned out, I was the most important contact he made. He came to the show, returned the next night and the ones after, invited me to dinner and fell in love with me.

He showered me with flowers and gifts and romantic meals, wooed me for three months before asking me to marry him. His overtures amused me at first, but I began to feel more, something I'd never experienced. I too was in love. And I had precisely the same reservations as you. Here's a rising star being groomed to follow in his father's footsteps. My William's wealthy and has this status. He's the American version of a nobleman. And he married me! Now do you see, *ma petite?*"

Her employer's revelations stunned the young Scot. A cabaret dancer? Well, that explained Patrice's grace and elegance of movement. Bella rose from her chair and wandered around the room, trying to assimilate what she had heard. A cabaret dancer who married an American 'noble' successfully. This last realization stopped her in her tracks. Patrice, the dancer, had successfully and happily married her prince!

The young Scot returned to sit beside Madame. She grabbed the older woman's hands and brought their faces near until their eyes searched each other's, demanding truth and truthfulness.

"Madame, do you mean I too can marry a man of aristocratic birth and be happy?"

"Yes, that's exactly what I mean! I have, *ma cherie,* why not you?"

Bella's practical side forced down the glimmer of hope. "How did you do it?"

"Remember, Bella, America isn't Europe. Fitting in would be much harder to achieve there. But here, class distinction is less strongly entrenched and is based on wealth. Sir David's title is important, but from what you've told me, he is rich enough on his own to be welcome in any social circle. San Francisco society will not judge you. You can do it, and I'll help you in any way you wish. We'll do it together, it'll be fun! Why? Because I look at you and see me."

Chapter 55

"Tam, bring me up to date on the Evening Star, will you? I haven't read your reports for weeks now and am completely out of touch." David had the grace to blush as he glossed over his drunken binge. "How's the new machinery behaving? Is it improving productivity?"

He was sitting by the creek in front of a campfire, warming up from his dip in the trout pool, while his friend shaved his beard. His hair was already strewn around his feet. As predicted, Tam's clothes were big for him but were presentable enough. He looked human again.

"Most of the equipment..." the older Scot launched into a long technical discussion of the benefits and faults of each machine. He also described the benefits and faults of each manufacturer, whom to believe and whom to distrust. Once more, his mentor's ability to absorb and master data far outside his knowledge left David awestruck.

Tam finally completed grooming his boss. "There you are, Sire, welcome to the land of the living. You can go into a zoo now without the apes swarming you!"

"Thanks Tam, you're a peach." David's spirits were approaching normal. "Let's pack up and be on our way. I'm keen to see Rush again."

Click. The sound of a gun being cocked.

Four more clicks.

The ex-soldier took a step upwind of the fire. His protege was judging the distance to the saddlebag holding his rifle. The five seconds of silence were an eternity.

"Buck Hall!" Tam called. "You had me worried for a moment. My compliments to your men, their woodcraft is excellent. I couldn't have done better myself. Come on out boys. There's coffee in the pot!"

The old Raider sidled out of the bush, followed by his two henchmen and the boys, Buggs and Caleb. David thought Tam had defused the immediate danger, but the primed weapons still pointed in their general direction.

"How did you know it was me?" Buck's ego was hurting.

"Your clothes reek of your pipe tobacco. I could smell it on the wind."

"Damn, I must be getting old. Guns down, boys." His crew obliged. David hid his sigh of relief.

"Why are you following us, Buck?" A legitimate question.

"Just makin' sure you don' bring more trouble on yerselves, Sir David."

"What do you mean? What trouble?"

"Your return today is a poorly kept secret. Every thief in the county's looking to pry your wallet loose. I'm here to protect you." Buck puffed up in self-importance.

Aye, and separate me from money too, I'll bet. "Okay, Buck, usual rates?"

"Thank you, Sir David. It's a deal."

Chapter 56

"**I**'d forgotten just how small Rush is when compared to San Francisco, Tam."

The two friends surveyed the mining town from a vantage point high above the river. What trees they could see on the other side of the Buffalo River were tinged with the green blush of spring's new buds struggling to emerge. No breeze today, so the smoke from the smelter hung in the valley like the gloom at a Scottish wake. The racket of the smelting machinery reverberated through the valley, drowning out the unfettered joy of the raggedy urchins playing among the slag heaps.

"Why aren't those children in school, Tam?"

"There is no school!"

David stared at his friend. "No school? Doesn't the church have a mandate to teach and convert?"

"There's no church either. Five weeks ago, a drunk set fire to the one you remember. The minister gave up and left. Rush's rougher than it was last fall when you were here."

"Hmmm." The Scot absorbed everything his mentor had to say. "What of the hotel - do we have rooms?"

"Yes, and rooms for the people taking part in the auction next week." Tam hesitated. "Sir David." The formality seemed appropriate. "May I ask why you're selling the Evening Star? Are you unhappy with the way it's being run?" Tam meant, was David unhappy with him.

The young noble saw the concern on his friend's face and hastened to reassure him. "No, no Tam, nothing like that. You're giving me exceptional returns on my investment and I'm thrilled with how you and John Williams are running the mine. You two are to be congratulated, which I will demonstrate soon with a handsome bonus. No, my desire to sell comes from the enjoyment I get... got... from living in San Francisco." A shadow crossed his eyes, and he sighed. "Despite Bella spurning me, I still wish to live there. I enjoy the atmosphere, and I find the business climate exhilarating. It has a vibrancy that I've never experienced before, not here and certainly not back in Scotland. California is at the center of the Pacific's universe and I crave to play a role in its development. The mine is too far away and requires too much of my time." He pulled himself up short. "But here I am prattling on and asking nothing of your life. How's Marthe?"

It was Tam's turn to lose his composure. The time which had elapsed from his encounter with the wild Irishman allowed him to laugh at his misfortune, and, in short order, he had David roaring in his saddle.

"Oh Tam, that's priceless, so it is!" he said, mimicking an Irish accent. "Let me be serious for a moment. Where does that leave you? When I decided to sell the Evening Star, I expected you'd stay here with Marthe and work for the new owners. Is that what you want?"

"No, Sir David. Marthe aside, Rush isn't big enough for both Rory and me. He's a good man and a good miner. I've got him running the second shift. But he's brooding and one night, when he's in his cups, he'll come looking for trouble. It's in his nature. That's unfortunate, he's a true asset, but there can be only one dog at the top of the heap, and that'll still be me. But he'd be a strong replacement for me after I've gone." Tam changed gears. "I'm glad to hear you want to put down roots on the west coast. If you need an extra hand, let me offer my services."

"Offer accepted, Tam. I miss your wise council, and judging from my 'Peking Duck' adventure, I'm not yet ready to be left to my own devices." The friends laughed, turned their horses, and trotted along the muddy road to Rush. Buck and his boys trooped after them.

Chapter 57

Stanley Chase, part owner of both the Evening Star and its neighbor, the Morning Star, was perturbed, a feeling he hadn't experienced since he'd last negotiated with Sir David Damnable Rennie. He was vexed; he was out of sorts; he was not in control and for a man who hated surprises, this was a most uncomfortable place. There had been several private talks between him and 'the whippersnapper' but his pleas for preferential treatment had fallen on deaf ears. David, as principal shareholder, remained adamant. The sale will be as honest as a Scottish Presbyterian minister.

"No, Mr. Chase, the auction will unfold as I described. I expect to have four companies submitting offers. The principals must be present and their proposals in writing and sealed. I'll open them and the top three bidders go on to the next round. They bid once more, and, again, I review the submissions and dismiss the bottom one, leaving two contenders. As soon as I inspect the final bids,

I declare the winner. At no time will I reveal any of the tenders."

"But, Sir David ..."

"No, Stanley. That is the way it's going to be."

"But ..."

"No 'buts'. I told you." David took pity on the mining executive. "Listen, I understand your eagerness to win the auction. Who wouldn't want to join the two properties? And you have backers who are counting on you. You must be under enormous pressure."

His co-owner nodded.

"Let's look at it from a different perspective. You're the majority shareholder in the Morning Star and a minority partner in the Evening Star. Even if your consortium doesn't submit the highest offer, the auction's going to make you richer than Midas. You might disappoint your sponsors, but business is business."

Stanley nodded, hiding his irritation with David for discerning the stress he was experiencing.

"Remember, you're already an insider. Your practical knowledge of the mine and the new vein is invaluable. You have information the other players can't glean from a mere report. Similarly, you know your workforce and how smoothly the operation runs."

The older man climbed out of his funk. "Talking of the labor pool, that's correct, they are productive, thanks to your friend, Tam. He's a born leader. But am I right to assume that both of you plan to leave Rush once the auction is complete? What'll happen to the workforce then?"

"Yes, we're heading to San Francisco but you'll inherit a well-oiled machine. Tam's likely replacement, Rory, is a strong, no-nonsense boss who will keep them in line. The miners will serve you well... assuming you leave their wages alone." He grinned, and even Chase cracked a vestige of a smile. They both knew the Scot was referring to the five-cent increase in the hourly wage he had instituted over Chase's outraged protest. David realized a new owner was likely to drop the higher rate, bringing trouble from the workers. It's easy to give a benefit, it's impossible to take one away.

"Rory will run a tight ship, Stanley. He and your engineer, John Williams, have got the experience necessary to manage the mines and the workers. That's another advantage you have, the other players are ignorant of Tam's plans. Don't worry, your investment will pay off handsomely."

Chase's guts churned. David's encouragement wasn't working.

Chapter 58

Auction day dawned clear, crisp and beautiful, a perfect spring morning. It was wasted on David; however, he could care less. His focus was on completing the sale of the Evening Star so he could return to his life in San Francisco.

Two of the bidders, Justin Roberts and Christof Temple, had arrived from California on Thursday. Ian Carlyle came on yesterday's train from the east coast. David soon found out they had a common trait: they all suffered serious deficiencies in morality.

Each investor took their host aside and offered him 'inducements' to sway the auction in his favor. David told each of them the same thing, "Nothing doing! And if you bring it up again, you're out of the auction." Carlyle ignored the threat and button-holed the nobleman after the Friday dinner, leading the young man outside to the deck encircling the hotel.

"Dave, I need information on what my competitors' bids are going to be. I want you to help

me, and I'll make it worth your while. Name a price."
David reached to grab him.

The charlatan backed away. "Calm down, my
friend, calm down."

"I'm not your friend and you're out of the auction.
Go tell that to your bosses!"

"I don't think so, son. Remember, you have a
sweetheart waiting for you in California. I'd hate to
see her come to any harm because of your rashness."

Carlyle smiled, it was an oily smile and the last
straw. The brawny young Scot seized him by the
collar of his jacket and the seat of his pants and
threw him over the railing as if tossing a sheaf
of corn. The investor landed on rocks fifteen feet
below, screaming in pain. The melee brought the
others from the dining room. Roberts had seen the
whole fracas and painted a blow-by-blow picture for
the other potential buyers. They hurried to distance
themselves from this madman, but the turn of events
also elated them; it meant one less bidder.

Tam sidled up to his colleague, a half-grin
splitting his beard. "Remind me not to get on your
bad side. You've a dangerously violent streak when
you're furious."

"Tam, what have I done? I almost killed someone." David was aghast at his own actions. He peered over the rail at the easterner.

"Knowing you, me lad, he said something to deserve it. What was it?"

"He threatened Bella."

"What? How did he know... Ah, I see. His company did its research. What did he say, laddie?"

The young Scot told him, his eyes going cold with the telling. "... and I'd do it again, no remorse."

The ex-soldier joined in the condemnation of Carlyle's threats, then added, "David, we have to put a stop to this now. I have a suggestion, if you're interested."

"Certainly, what's your idea?" They watched as the house staff helped the whimpering Carlyle to a bench. He looked bruised but not broken.

"We must isolate him until we can confront his bosses. What if we send him for a six-month working vacation at the mine where Thomas is stranded?"

"Excellent solution, Tam, I like it! That'll keep him quarantined until the sale is over and we're back in San Francisco. Buck will help... for a fee!"

*   *   *

The auction started at noon with the remaining three candidates, Chase, Roberts and Templeton.

It was over in less than five minutes.

David called the group to order and recapped the rules. He reminded the threesome of the stellar financial results that the neighboring Evening Star had achieved the previous year. He then summarized the assay report describing the new vein's potential. He caught the glances between the two west coast investors, raising his suspicions.

Tam collected the envelopes containing the initial tenders and gave them to David who opened each of them, perused the contents, and placed them face down on the table. Chase was straining his neck hoping to glimpse what his opponents had written, but to no avail. Neither Templeton nor Roberts showed the same level of curiosity.

"Gentlemen," David began, although he thought that was an exaggeration. "I strongly suspect there has been collusion between Messrs. Roberts and Templeton. Their bids are precisely the same. I presume your intention is to force Mr. Chase out with this high offer?" The miscreants avoided David's stare by examining their shoelaces. "Then you can compete against each other in the final bidding... at a lower price, of course." He scowled at the pair who were struggling to appear innocent. "Your bid is excessive, which, under normal circumstances, would guarantee that you win this round."

The silence was complete. The interlopers could hear the "but" coming from a mile away. David obliged.

"But Mr. Chase's is higher." Gasps from everyone. "If you remember, the lowest bidder drops out. As both submissions are lower and both the same amount, both of you drop out."

Pandemonium reigned with the outbid pair screaming at David, and attempting to do him bodily harm, Chase cracking a glimmer of a smile and Tam protecting his protégé, who was enjoying every moment!

Tam cleared the room, none too gently, and not without threats of dire retribution from the losing bidders. He leaned against the door. David grinned at him.

"Old friend, pour me a beer, please. No hard stuff for me, yet. Won't you join me?"

Tam strode over to the well-stocked sideboard, poured two ales and tendered a glass to his onetime student. "Where to next, David? San Francisco?"

"First I've to go to New York and execute the paperwork for the sale. Then to Frisco to change Bella's mind. We'll leave tomorrow."

Chapter 59

"Sir David! There's a letter for you.

It's from Bella!"

Chapter 60

Bella was enjoying high tea with her employer and now friend, Patrice Steben. The four o'clock snack had become a regular occurrence as social boundaries between the two continued to fade. They were seated in the Steben household conservatory high in the hills, relishing the weak sunshine as it fought a losing battle against the onslaught of the late afternoon fog.

Patrice pointed out and named the fresh spring growth for Bella's benefit while the children played their favorite game of marbles. But the tutor's focus was elsewhere. Patrice turned towards her with mock exasperation.

"Bella, you haven't heard a word I've said. This is not an iceplant, it's a dandelion. What's got into you today?"

"I'm so sorry, Madame. You're right, I am distracted. It's, ah, David..." She smiled contritely at her patron.

"Aha! I thought you had more on your mind than iceplants." her friend chided with a hint of laughter. "Good news, I hope?"

"I believe so. You know I sent him a letter?"

"You told me, *ma cherie.* Has he replied?"

"Yes, I received a telegram this morning telling me he'll be back in San Francisco this week. Oh, I can't wait to see him!"

Patrice smiled at Bella's naïve enthusiasm. "Well, we'd better examine my closet to find an outfit suitable for you to wear when your hero returns. And early to bed tonight so you can look your best!"

"*Bien sur! Oui, madame!"* Bella dipped a mock curtsy.

Chapter 61

David stared at the ceiling of the spacious bedroom in "Ballboyne West" as he had christened his purchase. His home stood high on the crest of the San Francisco hills, commanding a magnificent view of the Pacific Ocean. He was exhausted, his month-long journey with Tam from Rush via New York had ended only hours ago. It was five AM, April 18th, 1906, yet he couldn't sleep because his stars were finally aligning.

A waiting telegram told him the paperwork and finances from the sale of the mine were complete. Another telegram informed him that the lawyers had finalized the acquisition of the timber tracts in northern California. A statement from his bank showed him to be a wealthy young man.

But it was the much-folded letter he had received from Bella before leaving Rush that kept him awake

My Dearest David,

As a woman, I reserve the right to change my mind and thus to change my answer to your question.

Yes! I will marry you, if you'll have me.

Yes, I've come full circle, and I'll tell you how that happened when next we're together. Meanwhile, suffice it to say, I hope your proposal still stands; I can't bear the thought of you having second thoughts. Please reply and let me know if our love is meant to be.

How long will you be in Rush? When will we see each other? Oh, David, I can't wait.

Your Love
Bella

The young Scot could recite the message by heart. He gave up on sleep, rose, dressed in his exercise tunic and shoes and went to the basement to try out his new gymnasium.

Tomorrow... today... he'd find his beloved and they'd plan their future.

Chapter 62

"Mortals plan, God laughs."

Yiddish Proverb

Chapter 63

At 5:18 AM,

the great San Francisco earthquake
struck with unparalleled violence.

To be continued...

Acknowledgements

*H*ighland Journey is the second book in *The Highland Trinity*. This book's very existence is due to the positive responses I received from the first book, *Highland Justice*. Thank you, everyone, we writers thrive on feedback, the good, the bad and the ugly. (I'm referring to the feedback, not the writers!)

My sincere appreciation goes to the Arkansas and Florida Writing Groups who allowed me entrance to their meetings. Their camaraderie and constructive support made this journey much easier and less lonely.

In Florida, my connection to these groups came through one person, Dawn Evans Radford. She is another force of nature (cf. June Jefferson in AR) who champions the cause of Literature in many ways, be it leading Memoir Classes or creating and supporting Reading Groups or Writing Groups etc.. I had the distinct pleasure of having her edit my manuscript. Please note the good grammar is hers, anything else is mine! Thank you, Dawn. You are appreciated.

Made in the USA
Coppell, TX
25 October 2021